WAITED SO LONG

J.M. DABNEY

HOSTILE WHISPERS PRESS

Hostile Whispers Press, LLC

ISBN: **978-1-947184-28-2**

Cover by: J.M. Dabney

Cover Image by: Golden Czermak (FuriousFotog)

Cover Model: Caylan Hughes

Edits by: AlternativEdits (Laura McNellis)

Proof Edit by: Stephanie Carrano

Cover content is for illustrative purposes only. Any person depicted on the cover is a model.

REMEMBER:

This book is a work of fiction. All characters, places, and events are from the author's imagination and should not be confused with fact. Any resemblance to persons, living or dead, events or places, is purely coincidental.

PLEASE BE ADVISED:

This book contains material that is only suitable for mature readers. It may contain scenes of a sexual nature and/or violence.

For my Readers

I can't thank everyone enough for their support in purchasing and reviewing my titles and most importantly for embracing my voices who are outside the norm.

Every Body is Worthy!

Special thanks to the people who've kicked my ass every time I think about giving up. Tracey, Stephanie, Meredith, Michelle, Laura and Jenn. I love my enablers and the unconditional support y'all show me.

BLURB

What happens when your best friend's son comes home and he's all grown up?

Devon Hoffman has a secret. He's wanted a Daddy all his own, but when you're pushing fifty, you're completely over the hill. Newly divorced and trying to be single again after an almost thirty-year relationship, he's lost and needs someone to ground him. Except he's anxious and his depression intensifies until Bern returns after leaving the service and the younger man suddenly takes an interest. Can he let his guard down and risk losing his best friend or should he do whatever is needed to keep his secret safe?

PROLOGUE

BERN

2009

I held on a few seconds longer than I should have, but except for leave, this would be the last time I saw Devon Hoffman. His smaller frame fit perfectly against mine. But the moment was bittersweet. I was allowed to hold him one last time. Devon's husband cleared his throat, and I barely restrained myself from shooting the man a death glare. Lawrence had never deserved Devon. I'd known that fact for years.

In a few minutes, I'd have to walk away from him for a second time to put the distance necessary between us. I was barely more than a teenager when I'd noticed how beautiful he was when he smiled. The musical quality of his laughter. I also knew how he shut down when his husband was too close. So that was the first time I'd had to walk away, and I ran all the way across the country to UVA in Virginia.

He was married, had pledged his life to one man for the past twenty years, and I couldn't compete with that. I released him but took the opportunity to stroke my hands across his lower back to his hips. My gaze caught his for a split second.

"You be careful."

"I will." I'd joined the military at twenty-one to put myself as far from temptation as I could get and I was leaving for boot camp. The need for him had been tearing my heart out because I couldn't have him. Outwardly, I'd understood my love for him was wrong. He was older and married, but my brain still screamed at me that he was mine. I'd never done more than hug him or watch him from a distance, and I hadn't given my inappropriate needs a voice. That didn't mean that every night since I figured it out I didn't live in a fantasy world where we were together.

"Take care of Dad for me?" I asked because I knew it would keep him close. I could ask my dad how he was doing and if he seemed okay. I didn't think his husband would physically harm him, but the emotional and mental abuse were just as detrimental.

"I promise. You'll be home before you know it."

I wanted to confess all the secrets I'd kept to myself. Tell Devon that he was mine and promise I could make him happy.

I was only twenty-one, but at fifteen, I'd known the older man was meant to be mine. Maybe it had been a childish fantasy of the beautiful older man. Yet, I didn't think so. I could see the toll his unhappy marriage was taking on him. He smiled less. No longer found joy in the things he loved.

Every second of the last six years, I'd studied everything about him. His likes and dislikes. The things he took the most happiness in, like the way he'd turn his face up to the sun as he tended his garden. His expression was always serene. I knew what that calmness looked like as it was destroyed by the slamming of a car door. And the way his body would deflate.

I'd bitten my tongue until it was raw. I was chunky and too tall with a baby face. People would say I was too young to know what love was, but I'd learned everything I needed by caring for him in the only ways I could.

I couldn't stay any longer. I turned my attention to my dad. His face was streaked with tears. It had just been the two of us for twenty years since my mom died. Leaving him alone pained me. I worried if he'd sleep if I wasn't there to tell him to or if he'd eat. He was lost without someone to make his life orderly. Mom had done that for him and I'd naturally taken over the role as soon as I realized what he needed.

Being a caretaker came naturally for me. I wanted the kind of love that still shined in my dad's eyes when he spoke of my mother years after we'd lost her. She'd been his everything. *His center. His comfort*. I craved to know even a sliver of what my parents felt for each other, but I knew it wasn't meant to be. I took one last look at Devon as I told my dad bye. Assured him I'd be fine, but he knew my trips home would be rare. He understood, and that's all I could ask, but he said he'd visit as much as possible.

I released my dad and picked up my bag and turned away. I refused to look back. Hoping the separation and the span of a country—maybe an ocean—would cure me of my unrequited love.

2018

I read the email repeatedly for the last ten minutes focusing on a single sentence in the short message. I'd just rolled from the bed and told the man there it was time for him to go. My phone signaled that I had an email, so I checked it. I was concerned for a moment as my dad only sent me an email once a week with a rundown of his and Devon's week. The subject line had important typed out in all capitals.

The man behind me pressed his lips to my back.

"I said it was time to go."

I barely heard him call me an asshole, and I didn't care about his opinion. I'd picked him up in a bar, and I couldn't even remember his name. To be honest, I hadn't given a damn. I'd just wanted to get off and now that it was over with, I had no interest in a repeat.

Nothing had changed in the years of separation I'd put between myself and Devon. I still dreamed of him and worried every day if he was okay. If he was being loved on or neglected, but I knew everything. Dad kept me up-to-date. The last few years, Dad suspected that Lawrence had been fucking around. He'd left Devon alone for trips and dinners with so-called friends. Devon had meals and spent more time with my dad than he did with his husband.

Lawrence asked for a divorce.

My heart sped in my chest. My boy was free. My boy could be mine.

The door of my apartment slammed, and I relaxed. I knew I wasn't in a relationship with Devon, but I still felt guiltier with every man I fucked. They were always a poor substitute for the one I needed. Months morphed into years, and with every year, I'd lost the tenuous hold on my hope he'd one day be free.

I started planning as I stood up and headed for the bathroom, then I sat my phone beside the sink. The man looking back at me wasn't the one who'd left. I had another year on my contract. I'd need to put in my papers saying I didn't want re-up for another tour.

I was older and harder. While I was happy with my choices, the years in the military had me starting to feel the weight of the expectations. The role I played to keep myself away from Devon.

I washed my face and cleaned myself up, wanting to rid myself of the stranger's scent. Then picked up my phone and called my dad.

"I knew you'd call as soon as you got it."

His voice didn't hold an ounce of judgment. We'd always promised to be honest with each other, and I'd confessed my feelings to him about Devon the day I experienced the first wave of the crush. Crush—that word lacked the intensity of what I'd felt. Obsession turned to love, then to heartbreak when I had to tell him goodbye.

"What happened?"

"Devon is kind of a mess. He just said Lawrence came home with the papers. Claimed he didn't want to be married anymore. Devon is lost at the moment. He's forty-seven, and after close to thirty years, you think you're in it for life."

"Is he staying with you?"

"No, Lawrence got an apartment and moved out a few days ago. I didn't know anything until Devon showed up tonight. I don't think it really hit him until Lawrence didn't come back. I put him in your old room to sleep here tonight. I knew that would satisfy your possessive nature."

For the first time in a long while, a true smile tugged at the corners of my mouth. I loved that Dad got it.

"I'm coming home, but it'll take a bit. You'll take care of him until I get there?"

"I've been taking care of him for you for a long time. A bit longer isn't going to hurt anything. You just do what you have to do. He's going to need some time to process before a bossy younger man makes his intentions known."

I agreed. I was his best friend's son. That wasn't going to be something easily accepted, especially after his long marriage ended. I'd tried not to hope too much, as time passed, I realized how small that spark of optimism had dimmed until I'd resigned myself to unhappiness in settling for a man who'd never completely take Devon's place.

"Just get home safe, and I'll make sure he's okay until you can take over."

"Thanks, Dad. I love you."

We spoke a few more minutes as Dad caught me up with his life and how he was doing. We said goodbye, and I disconnected the call. Everything I needed to do was playing through my head, but more than that, I was wondering what Devon would think about his soon-to-be Daddy coming home?

1

DEVON

2019

My chest tightened as the panic took over, and I popped another pill to bring myself from the edge before I tipped over into the scary abyss of my newfound anxiety. Only six months had passed since the ink had dried on the divorce papers ending my twenty-year marriage, but we'd been together for nearly thirty years. He was my one and only. I'd met him in my senior year of high school and had visited colleges. I'd met him at a club and hadn't come out yet. The excitement of my first boy kiss had clouded my judgment. I'd gone home with him that night. It wasn't an enjoyable first time, but I'd figured as firsts went, it wasn't terrible. We'd started seeing each other when I could sneak up for weekends and then I'd moved there for college.

It all had seemed like a fairy tale at the beginning. But as years lapsed, I felt the weight of what I'd done. I might not have liked it, yet my parents told me relationships take work. Slowly I came to realize that all the work in the world wouldn't make my once loving husband want me again. My gut told me he'd gone outside our marriage for sex. I hadn't minded, I'd had my secrets too.

In moments of weakness, I'd tried to analyze what I'd done wrong—if I could've done something different? If the sex had turned too routine? A week ago, I'd walked into what had been our favorite restaurant and found him dining with someone else.

The man was close to our age, and from their body language, there was nothing friendly about it. I'd almost left without getting my food in case he'd noticed me and my dinner for one. I didn't know why it bothered me so much. Yes, I'd noticed we'd started to grow apart but wasn't that how it was with most couples who'd been together decades—it was natural. Lawrence was always the outgoing one, gym five mornings a week, and wanting to be out every weekend. I was the homebody partner. Dinner at home and curling up on the couch to cuddle.

While I missed my marriage, it was more about the companionship that I no longer had. Our sex life hadn't satisfied me. I was embarrassed about my fantasies and had refused to ask for what I wanted. And I was too old to be some Daddy's boy. I wanted someone to love and protect me, guide and ground me. I wanted to be owned by someone.

"Dev, are you okay?"

I lifted my head to find my best friend, Murray, peeking out the back door to where I was seated at the patio table. His presence reminded me of why I was there. Bernard, or Bern as he was known, was coming home. I hadn't seen him in six years as he'd joined the Marines right out of college. I always seemed to be away on business when he'd come home on leave. I remembered he'd been a sweet-natured boy, always tall for his age and chunky. Because of my traveling schedule, I hadn't spent a lot of time around him, but Lawrence had always said Bern was a weird kid. Said he was rude, but I'd always found him to be super polite. Always ready to help me with yard work or random chores Lawrence had claimed he didn't have time to do.

"Yeah, is he here yet?"

"Just pulled in. Come on."

I chuckled at my best friend's excitement. Murray had been a single dad since his wife had passed away from cancer when Bern was only a year old. Murray had been friends with my ex, and I was just glad I got to keep him in the divorce. All the other friends Lawrence and I shared went with him. I pushed to my feet and made my way inside, losing sight of him as he disappeared out the front door. When I stepped outside, I froze at the scene playing out. A massive brute had Murray off his feet and hugging the life out of him. That couldn't be Bern.

Then Murray was back on his feet, and I was the recipient of a huge smile. I almost backed up when he came toward me, but I receive a hug from the muscular man, just not one as manly as Murray got.

"Devon, Dad didn't say you were going to be here." That voice was guttural like gravel abrading together. Almost frightening. Where the hell was the boy I'd known?

I didn't know what the hell to do. "Welcome home. Murray called me yesterday and said you were home."

"Finally. Dammit, Dad, I got it."

Bern ran off to pick up the bags Murray was struggling to carry. He easily hefted them from the older man, and he was headed in my direction. He stopped a few feet from me. "Go on." He smirked at me as he did this gentlemanly bow and sweeping his arm to motion me inside.

I took the steps still in shock. Bern wasn't the cute, chubby kid I remember when I went to his college graduation. He was muscles on top of muscles, and gritty, dangerous voice. I was feeling a lot older than I did ten minutes earlier. He had a beard for fuck's sake. Pills or not, I needed a drink.

"Quit fussing around. I'm home for good, so you can worry about me in a few days."

Murray was a bit anxious all the time. Quick to lose himself when he became overwhelmed. It hadn't been that way when Bern's mother was alive. She'd always been able to get him to focus and calm him. Bern had taken over that job when he'd gotten old enough to realize his dad was a bit spacey. Murray and I were both a mess. It was no wonder we remained friends.

Instead of the drink I wanted, I grabbed a bottle of water and leaned back against the counter. I smiled as the younger man got his dad settled with a beer and then grabbed one for himself. Murray suddenly had a sereneness around him. Bern favored his mother. The same ginger curls and blue eyes. I remember she was constantly smiling. Even at her lowest, she'd held it together for Murray and Bern. She'd lived longer than the doctors had said she would. I'd been in awe of her. I think the only thing that kept him going after she died was he had Bern—the mini version of her.

Instead of feeling left out as they spoke in whispers on the other side of the island, I was relaxed and enjoying my friend having his son back. Emails, letters, and video calls weren't enough. I was happy Bern was home and had put Murray's mind at ease.

"I better make dinner."

When Murray tried to stand up, Bern pushed him back down onto the stool and wrapped his arm around his dad. "Dad, you just sit and relax. Have your beer. Unless you want dinner, in that case, I'll make it."

"You just got home, son."

"Ain't got shit to do with it. You want me to make dinner? Devon, you hungry?"

Those bright blue eyes focused on me, and I felt exposed under his intense stare. I wondered if I'd doubled my anxiety meds because something was off with me today.

"No, I had a late lunch. I think I'm going to head home. I leave for a business trip in a few days. There's a lot to do before I head for the airport."

"You'll give me your number so I can check on you while you're gone."

Even though the demand was clear in his voice, I wanted to say no. Yet, I also wanted to obey. My ex hadn't bothered checking on me while I was away on business. Maybe every few days I'd called him to say goodnight. Check in to see if everything was good at home, but I'd never felt compelled to contact him because I knew it probably wouldn't have mattered to him. He wasn't interested in my company, and I'd comprehended it too late. I realized I was staring at Bern, and he raised his brow as if expecting an answer.

"That's not necessary, I've been—"

"I don't think I asked if it was necessary."

I frowned at his tone and how his voice was even deeper, which I felt should be impossible. It was commanding and comforting but not the same tone he'd used with Murray. It was hard and unyielding. An order pure and simple. I didn't like conflict, so I felt my only option was to agree.

"Um, okay."

"Good boy. You'll be here for dinner tomorrow night. Six o'clock."

All I could do was nod, and then I was saying goodbye as I headed for the door. Bern had changed a lot more than just physically since he'd left. The shy boy I remembered was no more, and I wasn't sure how to handle the stranger who returned.

. . .

I LOCKED MYSELF IN MY HOUSE AND WENT TO TAKE care of emails and study my itinerary. I could retire, but what would I do with myself? At least work kept me busy. It distracted me from the loneliness. I worked because I had nothing left.

I took a seat at my drafting table as I worked on the new design for my client. His steel monstrosity would clash with everything around the building. It was a showpiece that had no more value than broadcasting his wealth. Once again, my brain went back to wondering if it was time to retire, maybe working for myself, but I felt I was too old to start over. All I felt was doubt and insecurity.

When I was younger, I'd felt confident and fearless. Every day was ripe with possibility, and now I weighed everything by what was expected of me. I felt as if my life was over with; I wasn't even fifty and hopelessness weighted me down. When I looked in the mirror, I could only see what I was and not what I could be. That, out of all the recent events, was the hardest reality to accept. I viewed myself through a skewed lens Lawrence had shaped.

My fantasies were still a cause of shame just as they were for the past thirty years. I'd forbidden myself from demanding what I wanted because what would people think when they knew the real me. The person who existed beneath the façade. The respectable architect in a small suburb who was just a shadow of his former self.

I was a middle-aged man with silver-streaked hair and a belly, who dreamed of the impossible. I tossed my pencil aside and got up. My mind wasn't in it, so a shower and early to bed. Tomorrow was a new day.

2

BERN

I made sure Dad was tucked in and settled for the night. He was trying to do too much. I knew he missed me, but I didn't want him trying to wait on me hand and foot. Dad needed more focus and someone to center him. My mom had been his Domme, and she'd made sure my dad had always felt confident and safe. When I'd gotten older and I realized what their relationship had been, I'd tried to get him to find someone else, but even decades later, my mom was all he'd wanted.

She'd been almost a decade younger than Dad when they'd met. He said she came up to him in a bar and said he was going to be hers, and that was the start of my parents' fairy tale. They waited five years before they'd had me. Growing up, I'd always made sure Dad was okay. That he ate, slept, and I made his life orderly so he never felt out of control. He always said I was just like her. My presence was calming. I didn't know about that. Plenty of people had called me weird growing up.

One was Devon's ex. I'd hated that man since I was fifteen and realized he had something I wanted. Lawrence hadn't treated him right. Inattentive and cold, taking him for granted. My feelings hadn't changed in the last thirteen years, but he had been married, and I had to respect that even if I loathed it. Three long years, I'd watched and had to standby as Lawrence became emotionally unavailable, not taking care of Devon as he deserved. I'd fucked because I was human and loved sex, but I always waited with hope that Devon would be free one day.

More than the occasional one-night stand was unacceptable. I'd refused to move on as if he didn't matter to me. What was I supposed to do? Pretend that the older man had never meant anything to me? That wouldn't happen. I knew people would think me strange that I put my life on hold for a man who was emotionally and physically unavailable. In my stubbornness, I refused to admit defeat. Lawrence would've fucked up sooner or later, and then Devon would be all mine.

My dad hadn't truly understood, but he respected my decisions. I never kept anything from my dad—honesty was important to a trusting relationship between anyone. He hadn't tried to talk me out of it because, as he always said, I was just like Mom. He knew of my feelings for Devon and stayed close to Devon for me. Dad had kept me up-to-date, emailed me as soon as Lawrence asked for the divorce and I'd put in my papers to come home. My years in the service had only kept me from longing for the boy I couldn't have. *Boy. Mine.* I wanted to be balls deep as he begged Daddy to fuck him harder. And now it was my time to care for my boy as he deserved.

I'd started the process when he'd come over for dinner last night. I held on a little longer than necessary when I greeted him with an embrace. Fixing his plate before I made mine. Touching him when I passed by. I'd memorized every time he leaned into my touch or the way his breath caught when I laid my hand on the small of his back. He felt something when I touched him; he just didn't understand yet what that was.

I grabbed my phone off my nightstand and scrolled through until I found Devon's number. I smiled, anticipating his surprise when I followed through with checking on him. For the time being, I knew I had to act with patience and get him used to being mine. The first step was making sure he took care of himself. I stretched out on my bed and connected the call.

"Hello."

Devon's voice was low and sweet. He was a small man who'd softened with age, and he was just as sexy as I'd remembered. "Hello, Devon. Tell me about your day."

"Bern, what are you doing calling me?"

"I told you I was going to call and check on you. Now, do as I said."

"I've only been here a few hours. I missed my connecting flight due to a mechanical delay and had to wait for the next one. I'm tired."

He sounded exhausted, but he'd looked it when I'd shown up a few days earlier. I hadn't planned on hugging him. He'd been close, and I wanted him in my arms even for an innocent hug. Touch formed intimacy and comfort, and he felt right in my arms. I'd always been taller than him and bigger than him. Years of lifting weights hadn't changed that...if anything I was even larger. Working out was required for my job. Yet it was also the way I exhausted myself enough to sleep because thoughts of him kept me awake.

"Have you eaten yet?"

"No."

"That I can't allow. I'll order you room service or call someplace else. What's your hotel and room number?"

He stuttered out an answer, and I knew he didn't understand why he was taking orders from his best friend's son.

He'd get it soon enough. When he came home from his business trip, we'd be spending a lot of time together. I think a first date is way past due.

"You know what I want you to do?"

"N-no."

"Get in the bath and relax. You had a stressful day, and I'll order you dinner to be delivered in an hour."

"Bern, you really don't have to. I'll probably just go to sleep."

"No, you need food and rest. If you won't take care of yourself, then I have to do it, boy."

"I'm not a boy, Bern."

Oh, he so was, but he didn't know what I knew. One day when I was seventeen, I'd finished mowing his lawn and put everything away, and on my way home, I'd stopped outside his bedroom window. I hadn't been able to see through the curtains, but I would've been jealous if I hadn't known Lawrence was at work. Devon had been inside whimpering. I heard the buzz of a vibrator, and as he came, in his pleasure, he'd gasped Daddy. I'd dreamed of being his Daddy. I didn't give a fuck if he was older, Daddy/little had nothing to do with age. It was a state of mind, and my boy needed me.

I'd gone home and jerked off to fucking him into the mattress, so hard that he felt me every time he sat down at work. Imprinting on him until touching his husband would feel like a betrayal to me. A year later, I'd left for college, and I'd missed him. While Dad gave me all the information, I wasn't there to make Devon feel safe as I'd learned Lawrence wasn't treating him right. Abuse was damaging, no matter how it was done. Emotional and mental abuse left as much a mark as a physical blow. The scars left behind didn't fade as easy as a bruise or mend like a properly set bone.

"Then don't act like a brat. Listen to me." I'd almost told him to listen to Daddy. It was too soon. Pushing him before he was ready would cause him to pull away from me. I couldn't have that. I'd waited years for him to be free and I wasn't going to do anything to fuck it up.

"I remember you being a lot sweeter before you left for college."

I grinned at the obvious pout in his voice. I was going to have so much fun making the bratty boy mine. And to me it was more than fucking him, Daddy and boy weren't just for our bedroom. I'd be his Daddy twenty-four-seven. I'd be his safety and comfort. I'd love on him but discipline him when needed. I nearly groaned imagining him laid across my lap as I spanked his ass.

"Bern? Are you still there?"

"Yes, sorry. Go take your bath, and I'll send you dinner."

"Thanks. I am hungry but too tired to go out."

"Then you do as I say…long hot bath, and then I'll make sure your belly is full."

"Okay."

He sounded so shy, and I sensed he was uncomfortable with something. I didn't like that I was making him insecure. "What's wrong? I can hear it in your voice."

"It's stupid."

"I won't ever think something you tell me is stupid, especially if it's something I can fix. So tell me."

"It's nice being taken care of. It's been rough lately, and long before the divorce. Things weren't good and…well, it's just nice to have someone else take over for a few."

"Baby boy, there's nothing stupid about what you said. I'm kinda bossy so get used to it. I'm not the same boy that left for college. You'll just have to get to know the new me."

"You're still sweet. Murray did an amazing job raising you."

I don't know why, but I felt he was trying to put distance

between us by mentioning Dad, soon I'd figure out if it was an unconscious maneuver.

"Yeah, he did. I don't remember Mom except for the stories he used to tell me. He was all I ever had. I want to thank you for taking care of him while I was gone. I picked up the phone to call or send you an email hundreds of times, but time always seemed to get away from me." It was partly the truth, I'd done both, and I always disconnected the call or erased the email. The moments always hit me late at night, when I was missing him and alone in my bed. I had to remember that while I'd wanted him almost half my life, he still saw me as Murray's kid. The always helpful boy next door.

"He wasn't all that much trouble. We just had dinner together a lot. His favorite subjects were you and your mom. I always wished I'd been lucky enough to have a love like Murray had for your mom."

"You know it's not that late. Lawrence was an idiot to not know what he had."

His chuckle was almost musical. "You're really good for my ego, but I'm fading fast."

"Then go do as I say, and I'll surprise you."

"Thank you, Bern."

"You're very welcome."

I reluctantly disconnected the call as I grabbed my laptop to search for restaurants in the area. I knew all my boy's favorites. He'd be shocked to know everything I'd learned about him. How often I'd watched him. At fifteen, I'd focused on him while my peers were fucking and getting high. I studied all the ways to make him happy for when it was finally my chance to own him. Even then, I'd taken every opportunity to touch and hug him, but he never noticed I was doing it. I'd given him gifts. He hadn't realized that I'd noticed it was something he'd looked at a few minutes longer or that I saw him open his mouth to say he loved it, but shut up when Lawrence hadn't looked interested or ignored him altogether. It was those little things that I'd tried to take note of because anyone can notice the obvious things. Someone who cares remembers the so-called insignificant details.

Pressing *complete purchase* for his dinner and chocolate for dessert because my boy had a weakness for sweets, I finished up and closed my laptop. I got off the bed and headed for my bathroom, stripping as I went. I caught sight of myself in the mirror. I didn't really study myself often. People either liked what they saw or they didn't.

My boy was on my mind, and his voice lingered in my head. I took the time to compare myself to Lawrence. He had spent almost three decades with the bastard. Lawrence was always smooth and polished. Elegant to the extreme.

I was six-five and nearly two-hundred and sixty pounds of bulky muscle. Where Lawrence was smooth, my chest was covered with a thick mat of auburn hair. I even had patches on my shoulders. I didn't groom or trim, so the bush at the base of my cock was thick. I was a big hairy man, and while I worked out, it was more about passing the time than an actual compulsion to do so. Lawrence and I were complete opposites. Devon didn't see me as a man yet, but I wondered what he'd think about me.

Closing my eyes, I brought up an image of Devon, wrapped my rough hand around my cock and stroked as the long length firmed under my touch. I was a man built to be proportionate, and I pictured my boy's hole strangling the girth. I growled as I flattened my free hand on the counter. My boy would suck my cock and nibble on the foreskin just like I needed, sucking the loose skin between his lips. I jacked my dick, not satisfied with beating off when my boy's mouth or ass would be so much better.

I grunted and growled as my sac started to draw up,

preparing to come, and in a matter of minutes, I threw my head back, shooting my load onto the cabinets under the sink. I breathed harshly through my nose as I massaged my length, teasing out every drop until my thighs shook. The release was fleeting because I knew that I wouldn't be happy until I filled my boy with my cum. Watching the satisfaction on his face as my seed leaked out of his ass.

Grabbing a dirty towel, I cleaned the cabinet doors and turned to start my shower. Devon would be home soon, but until then, I'd call and check on him, show him that his happiness was all that mattered to me.

3

DEVON

I was working in my company's local office, but something was wrong with my brain. My body had developed a mind of its own. I tried to focus on the new changes my client had notated on the last one. Every time he found some fault. Sometimes it was the tiniest detail, or like the previous design, he wanted a window moved an inch. If he wasn't such an asshole, I would probably appreciate his exceptional good looks. But my ex was handsome too, and he'd turned into a massive bastard.

I used the eraser to take out a line I'd mistakenly made while drifting off. Something I hadn't thought of since my divorce was the fact that I was single. I knew at my age I was way past my prime and not particularly on the hit list. Ageism was rampant among men, straight or gay. When men reached a certain age for some reason, they started looking at something younger with a tighter body. I didn't even know what the hell I was going to do.

I'd been on a handful of dates in my life. I'd hated it. When I'd met Lawrence, we'd seemed to be on the same level. On our second date, we'd discussed that we both wanted to settle down one day. My parents had instilled in me that you waited for the right one—the one you wanted to marry. I felt comfortable in a monogamous relationship. Except I was also jealous of the people who were freer and more open about sex.

For a minute last night, I'd almost gone down to the hotel bar. A constant buzz of arousal tingled under my skin. I'd awakened that morning reaching for my already hard cock—the remnants of my dream fading before I could capture the details. I felt slightly uncomfortable afterward as if I'd done something wrong.

Desire was building inside of me causing this jitteriness I'd never had before. Over the last five years, sex had gone from a chore—an itch to scratch—to non-existent. Lawrence hadn't seemed to want to touch me. I'd grown used to feeling as if I were sleeping alone. He hadn't even tried to cuddle with me at night. Those surprise kisses from early in our relationship had disappeared, and he wouldn't even hold my hand in public.

Yes, I missed the unrestrained need of twenty-something me who'd felt as if I was desired. But more than that, I yearned to be cared for, and with that thought, Bern popped into my head. I'd felt shocked when I'd answered the phone and heard his guttural voice in my ear.

I knew it was only because he'd known me all his life, and since he was a man now, I could consider him a friend. Yet, there was a forbidden thrill I'd taken in him ordering me to take a bath. Him sending me my favorite foods. My bruised, middle-aged ego took an instant liking to it.

In ways, it was like all those dreams I'd given up on over the last decade. I learned early to settle for what I could get. I'd believed myself in love with my husband, but that love turned so easily into complacency. Asking for what I wanted in and out of bed had tripped and frozen on the tip of my tongue.

I tossed my pencil aside and stood up from the stool. I walked to the wall of glass and the cityscape beyond. Loneliness was something I accepted as my due for a nice, comfortable life. I believed in freedom for all, and yet I couldn't let go of the expectations in which I was imprisoned.

I felt my cheeks flush as the needs I ignored came to the forefront. I wanted to be taken care of by a man who knew who he was. Someone dominant and strong. I wanted to be loved and fucked with equal measure. To have the weight of decisions taken from my shoulders. At the possibility of having that man who could ground me and push me, I felt tears burn my eyes. It would probably be more than I could accept.

Being a submissive was right there, I'd silently accepted it, but without a Dominant, over time, I became lost. The older I became, the easier it was to ignore that part of me. I was content when I belonged to someone, or so I thought. Lawrence hadn't had that possessive nature that urged him to stake his claim—let everyone know that I belonged to him.

I shoved my hands into my pockets and leaned my forehead on the cool glass as I was staring down in the brightly lit street below. All the issues I'd tried to push aside since Lawrence had served me with the papers started to spin through my mind.

When I learned that I'd become nothing more than a body to use—a tool for masturbation. When Lawrence had fucked me, his eyes were closed, and I knew deep in my soul that I wasn't the one he was seeing. The only time I felt any satisfaction was when I got myself off. I could imagine anyone and anything. My fantasy man calling me boy in my ear. I could give myself that bite of pain I needed, but it was still not enough.

Nothing was ever enough. Everything in my life had dimmed as the shine wore off. I was older and my body not as slim as it used to be. The threads of silver in my hair and the deepening creases beside my eyes showed me that my days of being someone's boy was long behind me.

I still didn't know how I was going to be a single, middle-aged man. I could date. Find myself someone new who might appreciate me, but I was too jaded and tired. I was no longer happy with life or my job. I'd always seen myself as a happy person. Except now I no longer felt like the man I used to be.

All I could think about were the what-ifs in life. What would have happened if I'd voiced that I was submissive? Would I have ended my fated-to-fail marriage before my husband had the chance? I'd seen it coming, but I'd thought if I just didn't let it solidify than I would be okay. I wouldn't be tortured by the memories of the subtle cruelty of the man I'd once loved.

I was so tired of being alone and unloved. I was starved for touch and desired to be possessed and allowed to give up control. Rationally I understood that people found love at my age and beyond, but those forbidden longings to be someone's boy—to call someone Daddy as they pushed me to the limits of what I felt I could handle seemed so out of reach.

My phone chimed and tore me from the plummeting landscape of my thoughts. I pulled my phone from my pocket and answered.

"Hello."

"Hi, Devon, tell me about your day."

I shivered at the obvious command in Bern's voice. I craved a man just like that. Maybe that's why I was losing my mind, an example of the type I wanted was right there to tease me with the impossibility. I did as he asked. Poured out each detail of my day as he responded and chuckled. Allowed me to experience what it was like to be important. I bitched about my newest project, and he validated my frustrations. It was novel and sweet, almost as if I no longer felt the weight of my existence suffocating me.

I focused on him while he talked as I paced the office. Just listening to him brought me peace and calm, something I'd so lacked. All I could do was hoard these moments. Savor and remember it to pull up later. Maybe I needed to really find myself. Go back to the times where I felt free and me, the young me who'd thought I'd had the world in the palm of my hand. I'd focused too much on what I'd lost with the divorce. Why not flip that and try to discover the things I'd learned or could learn.

Again, I relished the lightness as we talked and he growled when he told me I shouldn't still be in the office. Ordered me to go back to my room and he'd order me something special for dinner. It was so bittersweet, the calmness that I felt at having my decisions made for me, but it wouldn't last, and I couldn't let it happen. Sooner or later, my little flirt with my submissiveness would come back to haunt me when the gorgeous younger man found a man as perfect as him.

"I have to finish this project."

"No, what you need to do is listen to me and take care of yourself."

"You know I'm old enough to be your dad, right?"

"Doesn't mean I won't put you over my knee for disobedience, boy."

I felt my eyes bulge at his tone and couldn't think of a retort. I was standing frozen like an idiot in the middle of the room completely speechless. And I was embarrassingly turned on by it. I needed to end the call. He was twenty-eight and my best friend's son. I couldn't ruin the one friendship I had left.

"I should go."

"You should pack up your work. When will you be in your room so I can—"

I zoned out as every part of me argued, my body wondering how grown up he was and my brain berating me for the image that formed. I gave him a time and quickly made my goodbye. My face flamed, but even as I said I wasn't going to do as he ordered, I packed up my bag and left the office. Maybe I was losing my mind, that was the only excuse I had.

4

BERN

I poured Dad a cup of coffee as he settled at the kitchen table to have breakfast. He'd done nothing but fuss at me since I got home about the fact that I wouldn't let him take care of me. He hadn't just been my dad growing up but also my best friend. When it was just the two of us for so long, leaning on each other, we'd developed a strong bond.

"How's the seduction going?"

I snorted as I picked up both mugs and strode to the table, sitting down to eat. I had errands to run before coming home and calling my boy. I still remembered the way Devon had gasped when I said I could put him over my knee. That was probably a low move, but I wanted to hear his reaction at least.

"Promising."

"You were always stubborn when it came to things you wanted."

"Do you have a problem with this? You'd accepted it when I told you years ago."

He set his fork on the side of his plate, took a long drink of his coffee, and I rolled my eyes at his procrastination ploy.

He'd told me enough times how my mother would handle him when he got bratty. My dad had the potential to be a world-class brat.

"You were fifteen. I assumed it was a crush. We've all had one on someone older. It's like a teen rite of passage. I hate that your crush made you leave."

"But you always told me that Mom told you you'd be hers the first night she'd met you."

That serene smile I loved to see on my dad's face always made an appearance when I mentioned Mom. I wish I'd had her around growing up and giving me advice.

"And I've always said you're exactly like her. But, Bern, you set your sights on a married man."

"Which he isn't anymore. I lived my life. Did things I enjoyed, but I always felt I was waiting for him. I hated watching him become so miserable, and all I wanted to do was make him smile."

"Your dominant nature peaked early."

I laughed as I stared at him. "It's only for him."

"Bern, I just want you to know that you can't play with him and not intend to keep him. Be sure about this. I know you're level-headed and have always known what you want out of life. Lawrence was cruel in his treatment of him. He starved Devon of the most basic things. It was so clear what he was doing, and Devon couldn't be oblivious enough that he didn't see it."

"Not a day has gone by that I haven't thought about him. Waking up each morning and hating that he wasn't beside me. Enraged that another man was touching him and then learning that he was being ignored. Starved for love. This isn't some whim. Nothing has changed about my feelings except that I want him more. I'm older, I've accepted who I am, and I want to be for him what Mom was for you."

He silently studied me, and I could see his mind working.

I watched the shifting of emotions in his blue eyes. Memories of a past he missed. The only woman he loved or ever would love, and I hated that he couldn't see that he could find someone else like her. I'd told him over the years, loving someone else wouldn't diminish what he'd felt for her, but he couldn't see it. I wanted that type of love, and I knew I could find it with Devon. He was everything I'd wanted and I one day wanted to see the same sereneness in his gaze when he thought of me like my dad did my mom.

"Your mom always had this way. Calm yet commanding. With one touch, she could drive all the darkness away. I'll never find that again."

"I don't agree, but I respect your thoughts on that."

He shook his head. "You sounded so much like your mother right then. We discussed everything. I trusted her to know what was best, but she always took my feelings into account."

"Did you have a Domme before her?"

"Oh no, I'd never even thought about a relationship like that in my life. My parents were very traditional. The man worked and made the decisions. Mom stayed home to raise the kids and take care of the house. Dad took her and us for granted and instilled in me and my brothers that women were subservient because they were weaker. I didn't like it, but that's the way I grew up."

"We've never talked about it before, but why don't I see my grandparents or uncles?"

"You know your mother was brought up in foster care, but my dad noticed things when I brought your mom home. He took offense at the way she took care of me. The way I'd sit beside her feet on the floor and lean my head on her knee. I loved when she combed her fingers through my hair." He closed his eyes as if bringing up the mental picture and sensation, and when he opened them, I saw the sadness there. "He found it disgusting that I deferred to her for decisions. He told me I wasn't a man and my brothers treated their wives just like Dad treated Mom, and saw it as nothing problematic. My mother looked twice her age because she was so beat down and miserable. Your mom showed me that I didn't have to accept that life. I couldn't subject you to it. When you came out as gay, I realized that they would've subjected you to so much if I'd tried to reconnect."

I hadn't even thought twice about coming out. My dad didn't even appear to react to the fact if someone was gay or not. His best friend was married to a man and never once had I heard a hesitation when introducing someone's spouse or partner. He'd made me so comfortable and secure, that I just told him one day and he gave me a hug and told me to have a good day at school.

"I'm not complaining."

"We made our own family. A safe and happy one."

"And that's why I want Devon. His happiness is my top priority."

"Just remember that. I won't try to talk you out of it. Devon deserves to be happy, and I'm sure you can do that. Now, eat your breakfast. I have to go to my studio, and you have a job interview."

Dad had turned to his art when he'd taken early retirement. A love my mom had encouraged when they'd gotten together. It was his way of connecting with her. He'd paint, and she'd curl up in a chair to watch. You could see the pride in her gaze when he'd had his first show. The picture still rested on the table next to his easel.

I ate my food that had cooled off as we talked. I had a job interview in a couple of hours. A friend of mine just started a construction company, and he was looking for some guys. I knew how to run the machinery, and I worked for his dad during the summers in high school and college. I figured I already had the job, but I wouldn't start until Monday, if I was offered the job. The weekend was for me and my boy.

One more day and then he'd be home. Until then, I'd call and talk to him, make sure he had everything he needed. I had so many plans and needed to go shopping. I was going to take my boy on our first date, and it had to be perfect. Patience was getting harder to come by because Devon was so close and free. Nothing was holding me back from claiming him.

I knew he wouldn't understand at first, and he might resist because of who I was. I'd be sympathetic and listen to his concerns. We'd need to talk about rules, limits, and expectations. I'd give him anything he needed even if that was just time to think because if he agreed to be mine, I wasn't letting him go.

5

DEVON

I worked my favorite toy slowly into my hole. The girth was almost too much to take, and I opened my legs wider, adding lube to my crease. I gasped loudly as another few inches slipped inside. This was the first time I'd tried to get off since my divorce, and I'd been horny for days. The teasing had started in the shower, and I'd had to get out because I wanted to be filled as I got myself off.

Whimpering like a slut as I forced the last three inches past my rim. I could only give myself the pain because my ex hadn't liked to get too sweaty. Shaking my head, I drove all thoughts of Lawrence from my head. I craved the weight of a big body on mine. I wanted to be handled roughly. Forced to submit, I wanted slow too, but I longed for what I'd never had.

I dug my heels into the mattress as I worked my ass along the nine, extra-thick inches of dildo. I refused to touch my dick just yet. I just wanted to lose myself in the burn of being filled. Bringing my toy on trips wasn't something I did, but I'd added it to my suitcase at the last minute. Its presence taunting me until need broke me after three days of denying myself an orgasm.

The well-lubed toy made nasty, slick sex sounds as the base connected with my hole. I rolled over to straddle a towel covered pile of pillows and held the base. I grunted at the sharp twinge as the angle changed, and I rode the length pinching my nipples. My head was thrown back, and I stroked my body, dug my blunt nails into my clenched thigh to keep from stroking my cock. It would be over too soon. I wanted to savor this even if it was just an orgasm by my own hand.

My sex drive had been non-existent for nearly a year, hell, longer than that and it was back with a vengeance. I nearly cried as my phone started ringing. *No!* I just needed a little longer. My client was making life difficult, and I ignored it as I fucked myself onto my dildo faster. It was fucking heaven, and the thick veined length tortured my gland. I felt my balls tightening. I was so close to getting off without even touching my cock.

I cursed louder as my phone went off again and there I sat on my toy, a sweaty, frustrated mess. I jerked my phone from the nightstand and checked the display. *Bern*. Then I noticed the missed call was from him too, and I got worried.

I quickly connected the call. "Is everything okay?" I started to lift myself off the pillow and then froze. The guttural laughter in my ear made me clench, and I sank back down on my toy. I bit my lip to conceal my moan.

"Hi, boy. Everything is fine. You know I call at this time to check on you."

Unexpectedly my heart started to pick up the pace again.

"Tell me about your day, baby boy."

I had to clear my throat before I could speak. I felt naughty as I realized I was rocking my hips as he spoke to me. My body felt as if I was racing toward a panic attack, but this was different. Desire I'd rarely experienced turned my blood to fire. I lowered my chin to my chest, seeing myself bare, and my little cock hard and leaking. The newness of it shocked me. A flash of Bern beneath me with his waist pushing my thighs wide, and I was filled by him. Shame infused every cell of my being, and suddenly, my desire fled—leaving me close to tears.

"Come on, baby, tell me."

I shivered from head to toe when he called me baby. It was so inappropriate. He was almost twenty years younger than me, and I wanted to call him Daddy so badly. He was commanding and caring. Every night since I arrived, he called me and ordered me dinner, but only after giving me time to bathe.

"What's wrong? You're quiet. Do I need to come get you?"

"No, no, I'm coming home tomorrow. My client is making a pain of himself, but I just have to make it through one more morning meeting."

A part of me I'd hidden shattered and I wanted this—this moment, taboo as it was, it was a single act I craved. And just for tonight, I wanted to take it for myself. I was proud that I kept my voice steady even as I started to fuck myself again. His voice belonged to the Daddy Bear of my dreams. I bit the inside of my cheek to help control the sounds threatening to be heard.

"You sure?"

I hummed an affirmative. I wanted Bern to keep talking to me. There was something wrong with me, but I couldn't control it. My body had taken over. All I wanted to do was come as he growled in my ear. I was nasty, and I pictured him spanking me for my actions.

"Want me to pick you up at the airport?"

I was having a hard time concentrating as my brain

wanted me to demand him call me baby or boy again. I bet his weight would push me into the mattress as he pounded—I shook my head as the images started to materialize. I'd seen the hair that peeked over the collar of his shirt. His hands would be strong around the back of my neck as I nuzzled his hairy chest as he used my ass...brutal and feral. Him losing all control as he owned my hole. I wanted to feel his cum fill me as he called me Daddy's good boy.

"Devon?" His tone was sharp, and I wondered how long he'd waited for me to answer. "Boy, what are you doing?"

"N-nothing, I think I'm just exhausted and stressed." I lied as I held tighter to the base and started riding the length faster—slammed my ass onto it and it took everything in me to keep my breathing normal. I wanted to beg him to keep talking. More than that, I wanted to be at home taking his cock instead of something that, in my imagination, could only be second best. I needed him to want me so much that he kept me naked so he could have access to my hole whenever he wanted it. I wanted to tell him that I was fucking myself as I talked to him. Maybe if I said something, I could listen to him tell me what he wanted to do to me. I could have him order me to perform for him. Hear him jacking his dick to thoughts of dominating me. If I could just open my mouth, we could watch each other.

"When you come home, I'll take care of you."

"You don't have to do that. I'm an adult." I lied again. I wanted to be his little with an intensity that frightened me. Every dream and fantasy I ever had existed in a man I shouldn't want, but in a matter of days, he'd completely broken my perception of the man I'd convinced myself I was to make my existence easier.

"Yeah, but everyone needs to be taken care of on occasion, and that ex of yours didn't know how to take care of you properly."

"And you do?"

"Little boy, are you challenging me?"

"No." I was shocked by the way my voice dipped lower, almost to a whisper. I was flirting with my best friend's son. I'd known Bern his entire life, but the boy who left wasn't the man who had returned.

"Would you be shocked to know I want to take you on a date when you come home?"

I grunted as I slammed down again and the shock of him wanting to take me on a date made me forget to conceal my whimper.

"Oh yeah, I was going to wait until I could ask you face to face, but I want you to think about it."

"Think about what?"

I regretted lifting completely and feeling the emptiness, I returned to my back and slammed the toy back inside.

"Do you want me to talk to you while you play with yourself? You haven't been hiding those sexy little whimpers."

"Talk to me, please." I felt brave because he wasn't here to see me. My middle-aged body not on display as I filled my ass. When I returned home, I'd avoid him. I wouldn't be able to meet his eyes after this. Yet beyond the humiliation I felt, I required his commands.

"While you're getting off for me, you'll let me hear it all, and you'll make sure you tell Daddy that it's his cock you want."

"Yes...Daddy." I clenched and loudly moaned at being able to say that single word. I didn't even care how he knew what I considered my shame.

"Oh, boy, you're making Daddy hard. I have nine inches of uncut cock for you to ride when you get home."

"Daddy," I screamed as I tortured my ass and I didn't hide one grunt or needy noise. He wanted them all.

"If you were here, I'd have you naked and stuffed with a

plug so that I could take your hole whenever I wanted."

"Do you want me, Daddy?" Insecurity leached into my pleasure, and I needed to hear him put me at ease, even if it was just him joking with the old man playing at boy.

"For years. Tell me what you're imagining."

"I'm on my back, and your weight is bearing me into the bed. You're so hairy. Your boy likes that."

"Take your Daddy's cock, little boy."

His voice filled my head as he ordered me to do as he wanted me—slam it in hard enough to hurt. He was the embodiment of everything I'd always wanted. "I'm gonna come." He was breathing hard and growling. I swore I heard him jacking his cock.

"Do it, boy. Daddy's almost there. I don't come until you do." I fumbled as I put him on speaker to free up my hand and with two strokes, I was screaming and calling him Daddy. All I could hear was fuck, and then I was shocked.

"Boy, your ass was made for my cum. Thirteen years I've been preparing to make you mine."

"What?" I was a cum-covered mess lying in an exhausted sprawl with my toy still partially filling my ass. My hole was repeatedly clenching in the aftermath. How could he want me so long and I not notice?

"Oh yeah, I'm still working my dick because it's never gonna be enough until you're in bed with me. Since I was fifteen, I knew I was going to own you. I hated that bastard who got to hold you, fuck you, but I knew he never gave it to you like I could. How could he not want to touch you constantly? Kiss you? Show everyone you were his?"

I was forced out of the safety of the barrier I'd formed around me. This was only destined to be a single forbidden interlude where the Daddy in my head had a voice—a presence. It wasn't supposed to be more than that, and he was thinking about owning me.

"I learned everything about you to make sure I could take care of you. Do you know I heard you jerking off one afternoon? You whimpered Daddy at the end, and I wanted to be that for you. You've been my boy since. I got off so hard when I went home.

"You've been my fantasy, dream, and it killed me. As soon as I knew you were free, I made sure I could come home to you."

I didn't understand why tears were filling my eyes, but I felt it to my soul that he wasn't fucking with me. I remember my teen years of crushing on older men. Yet, they had all just been jerk-off fantasies. I never thought about them any other time. When I was fifteen, I'd seen my parents' neighbors fucking, one of the guys was huge and hairy. That was where my obsession began, but I'd never been brave enough to accept it. It was always my dirty little secret.

"You came home for me?"

"Yes, I couldn't be there knowing I had to watch you with him. Me in bed alone while someone else was feet away with the right to love on you. Don't get me wrong, I want to fuck you until you can't sit right, but I want to love on you. Hours of touching. Cuddled with my boy on my lap. You're mine. Now, you have to think long and hard if you want to accept that. I'm possessive and dominating. I'll want my way, but no one will ever love you as much as I do. Making you happy is my one and only goal in life."

I didn't know what to say, and I suddenly felt exposed to the point of roughly removing my toy and covering myself with the corner of the blanket. He spoke such pretty words, but years of neglect made me cautious. His promises were too sweet for me to accept.

"Baby, I can sense you're scared, but when you come home, we'll go on a date. I want you to get to know the man I am. Want you to see that I'm not lying but only time will do that. I need a shower, dried cum in stomach hair isn't comfortable. I want you to get some rest because you're coming home to me tomorrow."

"Bern."

"You know you want to say it. Just say it."

"Daddy," I whispered the word and marveled at the freedom I felt. As if decades of weight lifted from my chest with a few syllables.

"Yes, baby?"

"Don't hurt me."

"There is plenty I want to experience with you, give you, and none of them has anything to do with hurting you. I've waited way too long."

I loved his gruff voice and the conviction I heard in it. I truly believed he wanted me, and that shocked me. Bern could have any man he wanted, and he freely admitted that it was me. No one had desired me in years. I'd always been lacking because of what I required. But I'd hidden those needs, and the opportunity was right there, offered freely to me.

"I'll be there when you get off the plane, and then we'll come home, I'll hold you, and you can ask me all the questions you want."

"Okay."

We spoke a few more minutes and then said goodnight. After I disconnected the call, I collapsed. I covered my face as I broke. Tears wetting my hands, and it wasn't grief—it was joy. Decades of misery fading away as I knew the man for me would be waiting for me tomorrow. My rational brain tried to tell me not to accept it so easily, but my heart wanted to believe that I'd finally be happy. I needed that belief that I wasn't too old to be wanted. *That I could love and be loved.* I just had to remember that in my past, I once had hope.

6

BERN

I forced myself not to pace and shoved my hands into my pockets. He'd be getting off his plane soon. I'd just heard his flight number called over the PA system. After last night when I'd heard him come for me, my impatience was at an all-time high. Anticipation had built up to this one moment, wanting that person you didn't think you'd ever have. I'd used his extra key that Dad kept to let myself in earlier to leave him presents and set up for our night together. I wanted everything to be perfect.

We wouldn't fuck tonight because we had issues to clear up, but I'd have him in my arms. Experience our first kiss. From my height, I could clearly see the gate, and I smiled as I spotted him. He looked exhausted, and I didn't like it. Tonight, he'd relax and let me take care of him. The moment he saw me waiting, I knew he was thinking about last night. His face turned the prettiest shade of pink.

I waited for him to approach me and I didn't like that he wasn't looking at me.

"Baby." I raised my hand to press my crooked fingers

beneath his smooth chin. "Did you miss me?" I asked as I lowered my head.

The closer our mouths got, the wider his eyes became. I pressed our lips together, and the lush curves gave under mine, and I couldn't keep my groan contained. I wrapped my arm around his waist and tugged him flush to me. The curve of his belly cushioning my dick, and it took everything in me to keep it under control.

"Fuck." I stroked my tongue across his mouth. "You taste so fucking good." I didn't give a fuck if anyone was staring or judging. I finally had my boy in my arms. And from his shivering, I knew he loved being there. "Let's get home. I got the living room all ready for us."

"You do?"

"I bought you some presents and made us a place to curl up and talk. Tonight is all about us getting to know each other again, and then you're sleeping next to me all night."

He whined, and I saw his eyes looked glassy. He was trying to hide it from me as he turned around.

"Baby, don't hide from me. Don't you want to spend the night with me?"

"Yes, Daddy."

"That sounds even better in person, and you blush so cute when you say it. You ready to go home?"

"Yes."

I didn't release him as I led him to pick up his luggage, and with that done, we made our way to my SUV. I had a plan for him before I buckled him in all safely. One kiss wasn't enough, and the one I wanted to give him wasn't appropriate to conduct in the middle of a terminal. He remained silent but didn't try to pull away from me once on our stroll across the parking lot. I hit the fob to unlock my vehicle, letting him go to stow his things in the back seat and then I opened the passenger door. Before he could climb up, I had my hand fisted in his hair, and his ass cheek clutched in the other.

I captured his mouth and kissed him with years of pent up need. He was clutching at me, his nails scoring the back of my neck as I lifted him to sit on the seat. I forced my way between his thighs and my slutty little boy rutted against my stomach. I bit at his lips, tugged his head back until his heavy-lidded gaze met mine. He was beautiful, and I didn't hesitate to tell him so. He tried to turn away. "No, you've always been beautiful to me. Sexy. My perfect boy."

"I can't be your boy. I'm too old."

"My little can be anyone I want him to be. It's all a state of mind. I want to make sure you're safe and cared for, know you're loved. I want you to know your happiness and comfort will always come first. You need a Daddy to ground you, and I'm the only one for that." I leaned in to kiss the tears from the lashes of one eye then the other. He was cuddled as close to me as he could get. "We're going to go home, and I'm going to make us dinner and let you decompress from work. This weekend we'll have our first date. I can take you out and show you off."

I loved his shy laugh and the way he observed me as I buckled him into the seat. Kissing him repeatedly until I could tear myself away from him. I closed the door and walked around, then got in the driver's seat. I pulled out of the parking lot and started for home. When we got on the highway, I laid my arm across the console and laced our fingers together. He trapped my forearm against his ribs and held tight to my hand as if I would take away my touch. I had no intention of ever doing that.

We kept up safe conversation, I asked about his trip and work, even though we spoke every night he'd been away. He mentioned a new project he was doing for a local LGBT Youth Center. He was donating the design and plans, then helping with fundraising for the rest of the project. With the topic away from his current work, he seemed to relax completely.

I'd missed the sound of his voice, and I sat back just to listen to him ramble. He needed to leave the architectural firm he worked for and go out on his own. I remembered him loving his job, but now it seemed a cause of more stress than it was worth, at least in my opinion.

I felt him tense as we pulled into his driveway. I wanted to ask what was going on in his head and put all his doubts to rest. That took time that I wasn't sure I could give him. Because of his traveling, we hadn't spent a lot of time together as I grew up, but I was still his best friend's son. He'd been there when I graduated high school and college, and when I'd headed to boot camp. His brain was devising all the reasons he couldn't or shouldn't be mine.

I'd waited so long for the chance and wasn't giving it up. I had to convince him he was my boy. Reluctantly, I removed my hand from his and put my vehicle in park. He started to reach for the handle. "No, I'll come around and get you."

He nodded but didn't break his silence, and I felt the weight of his doubts as if they were mine. I got out, ran around to the passenger side, removed his luggage, then opened his door. Extended my hand and waited for him to take it. I enjoyed his shyness and sweetness. He might think he was too old to belong to me, but I had no worries.

"Should you go home to check on Murray?"

He tripped as he stepped down and fell against me. I caught him to steady him.

"No, he's off with friends for dinner and might be out late." I didn't tell him that Murray was invited to a party by

Lawrence. He'd wanted to decline the invitation, but I'd found it suspect that he'd called after months of no contact. Dad was going to satisfy our curiosity.

I placed my hand on the small of his back and nudged him forward as I carried his bags in. His hands shook as he tried to unlock his door, and I felt an odd mixture of amusement and guilt that I made him react that way. I wanted him to be completely comfortable with me. Finally, he got the key in the knob and was opening the door, he stepped inside, and I noticed the minute he spotted the nest of pillows and blankets on the floor. His favorite red wine ready to open. His snack waited in the fridge.

I kicked the door shut behind me, and he jumped, turning to face me.

"Baby boy?"

"Y-yes...Daddy?"

I set his bags in front of the table next to the door and tossed my phone and the contents of my pockets into the ceramic bowl on top of it to join his.

"Daddy made you a snack. Go get it from the fridge while I get everything ready." He was shocked by my dismissal, but it was safer to send him away. As much as I wanted him, I needed to show him what his life would be like from now on. I watched him until he disappeared, and I started moving around the living room. I picked up the box of his new toys and placed them next to the small chest for him to put away later.

Just as he reappeared with his plate, I was lifting his new teddy bear onto one of the chairs. It was huge and big enough for my baby boy to cuddle and hump.

"Daddy?"

I remained silent as I opened the wine, poured him a glass, and then I sat on the couch, never taking my gaze from him and the way he was staring at his new bear. “Come sit on Daddy’s lap.”

“Is that for me?” He released the plate with one hand and pointed at the stuffed animal.

“Yes. Daddy’s going to let you have playtime later, but first, we have to talk.”

He approached me and lowered himself onto my thigh, and he almost dropped his plate. I grabbed it before he could spill the contents. He was shaking so hard he was practically vibrating on my lap.

“First, we have to put your fears to rest. I don’t like my little boy feeling so anxious around Daddy.” I soothingly rubbed his back as he picked at the food I’d made him. “Tell me what’s wrong. I already said if I don’t know, I can’t make my boy feel better.”

“Are you playing with me? Like tomorrow, after you get me to do all these things, will it be like a joke?”

I took the plate and leaned forward to place it on the table. When I relaxed into the cushions, I looked at him. “Straddle Daddy’s lap. Now, boy.”

“Don’t be mad.”

“I’m not, but you’re asking to be spanked and sent to bed without getting to play.”

"Why do you want me?"

I raised my hands and cupped his jaw in my hands—stroked my thumbs along his cheekbones. "I waited so long to touch you like I wanted to." I whispered the words in a reverent tone as I closed the distance between our mouths, kissing him tenderly. I didn't take it further than that. He leaned into my touch.

"I remember the first time I thought you were beautiful. I'd always liked you. You came to my games and all that, it was nice, and I thought about trying to set you up with Dad."

"You thought about setting me up with your straight dad?"

"I was fifteen, and my Dad had more gay friends than straight, so it wasn't a big deal. So I started studying you, seeing what you liked so I could kinda mention things to him. Then I realized that I didn't want to share. I became a resentful asshole to Lawrence, but only when you weren't around.

"You came home from a business trip one summer, and we were having a barbecue. He was already there, and you showed up. You came out the back door with a cute smile. He didn't even acknowledge you, and I saw you deflate. When you approached him, he didn't think about touching you—kissing you. At fifteen, I was already taller and broader than you, and when he didn't hug you, I did. It was absolutely perfect. It became my mission after that to always make you smile."

"That's why you did it?"

I nodded.

"I never thought anything of it. You were always affectionate with your dad."

"I knew you didn't see me like I wanted, but that didn't matter to me." I drew my hands from where I'd rested them on his shoulders, then down his chest and to his hips. He arched into my touch, and I was sure he didn't realize he was doing it. He was so starved to be loved on that he was responsive to whatever I gave him. "Your misery grew over the years, and all I wanted was to make things lighter, to see you smile. I succeeded in a way."

"Did you leave because of me?"

"Yeah. Dad knew and semi-understood. I was eighteen and a legal adult, and yet, you were still married. But, fuck, how I wanted to own you. I used to dream you wanted me too and that we had to sneak around to be together. My teenage brain created this whole fantasy life, and in the end, you left him for me."

"That's like weirdly cute."

I chuckled as he tried but failed to hide his smile. Almost like I'd be mad if he was amused at my expense. "It wasn't cute when I was pounding you into my mattress every night." I leaned forward until I could place my lips against his ear. "And then I learned your secret," I whispered.

He draped his arms over my shoulders, and his breath warmed the side of my neck.

"Since I did, every jerk-off session has ended with you whimpering Daddy in my ear. I learned everything to make sure your needs were always met. I want nothing more than to be your Daddy. Go on a date with me, boy."

"Yes, Daddy."

"Good boy. Do you want to play before we have dinner?"

"Play?"

I eased him off my lap and laid his bear in front of the TV. "I want you to play with your new bear. Strip down to your underwear."

He awkwardly did as I ordered. I returned to my seat on the couch. I was pretending to casually observe him as I turned on the television and looked for something to watch—more for background noise. The teddy bear was extra-large and fluffy. He straddled it and rested his full weight on it. When he hugged its neck, I thought he was just settling in to have a moment to think over what we'd spoken about, but then I noticed the small movements of his hips. I could barely tell he was humping his new stuffy. His whimpers were muffled by it. I adjusted my cock as I settled in to watch him, take note of how he moved, and I tried to relax my shoulders.

It was harder to resist him than I initially thought. He kept riding the stuffed animal until I saw him stop moving. I smiled at his soft snores. My boy was exhausted. I'd let him have his nap but not a long one, or he wouldn't want to be put to bed later. I wanted my boy to feel secure with me, and hopefully, a comfort item would help him. After our date was soon enough to take it to the next phase of claiming ownership of him.

7

DEVON

I was a nervous wreck as I prepared for my date with Bern—my first since my late teens. I'd taken extra time in the shower to get ready for the night. The clothes I chose were safe, navy slacks and a blue button-down shirt that everyone complimented me on when I wore the color. The dress shoes were the ones I sported for business meetings. I agonized over whether to wear a tie or not.

He wouldn't tell me where he was taking me or anything we'd do. Every time I'd asked the last few days, he kissed me and told me to be patient. I smiled to myself and caught the sight of it in the mirror. The harshness of my features from the last few years had faded as if they'd never existed. He popped over at odd times during the day just to kiss me, smirk and walk away. It was as if I was constantly on edge, but not in a bad way.

He called me every night just to tell me goodnight and that he'd missed me, no matter if he'd seen me ten minutes earlier or not. To be honest, I was still overwhelmed by all of it. I'd grown used to Lawrence's disinterest in me. Accepted it was my fate until death do us part.

Bern didn't make me feel as if I was going through the typical mid-life crisis of wanting a younger man. He was very much the dominant one, and I was loving the beginning stages of embracing my submissiveness. The freedom was exhilarating. He'd even ordered me to place my new toy box on the couch for when we got home, and I was so nervous about what he was going to do with me.

The doorbell rang, and I didn't want to keep him waiting. I grabbed my jacket from the foot of my bed and paused as I wondered if he'd share the bed with me again. The night I'd returned home, we'd talked about ourselves. I got to know the man Bern was now, and I loved what I heard. He'd given me a comfort item. I'd felt naughty as I'd humped my teddy while I pretended to watch whatever show he'd put on. I'd been so relaxed I'd fallen asleep on it.

But the best part was he'd carried me upstairs after he'd fed me, drew me a bath, and washed me. Afterward, he'd tucked me into bed and curled up beside me. It was the first time I'd cuddled with a man all night. I'd loathed the feel of his clothes against my bare skin, and when I pouted, trying to get him to strip down, he'd denied me. Told me to be a good boy and he'd make sure I received a reward.

The sound of him ringing again made me run downstairs pulling on my jacket. I rushed to the door and opened it, freezing as I looked up at him. He was dressed similar to me. The top two buttons of his shirt were undone to show off the thick hair on his chest. I knew exactly what it felt like when I nuzzled into his chest as I woke up.

He stepped inside, grabbing my face and tipping my head back with his thumbs beneath my chin. He captured my lips with his and kissed me gently until I was lifting onto my toes to get closer. “You look gorgeous.”

I wanted to protest his compliment but knew he'd be upset with me, and I didn't want that. I wanted my Daddy to be proud of me as his boy. “Thank you. You look very handsome.”

“Glad you think so. You ready to go?”

I hated when he let me go but tried to hide it. I collected my keys and wallet and smiled up at him as I realized he kept close to me. Never more than several inches away.

“What made you smile, so I make sure I do it again?”

My smile widened, and my cheeks started to hurt. I'd been skeptical about Bern’s interest after the phone sex incident and thought he was just having fun at my expense. Since I'd returned home, he'd proven that wasn't the case. Yet, I still didn't want to hope too much and get crushed in the end.

"You're never out of touching range."

"I'd have you in my arms right now, but I promised myself I was going to do this right."

I didn't know how to respond because again it was all so much. He took my keys, nudged me outside, and locked the door behind us. He did all the things that made the start of a date perfect or at least what I thought how a date should begin. I loved the gentleman routine, but only because it was genuine. He performed the actions not as a practiced act but as something he naturally did. And I had to admit that I liked when he opened the door for me. Buckled my seat belt to ensure I was safe. Gave me quick kisses between each step.

Maybe there was something wrong with my obsession with someone taking care of me. Perhaps obsession wasn't the right word. I'd dreamed of it so long that I wanted it to continue. I didn't feel weaker when he took care of me. I felt cherished and wanted, as if he truly believed that I was the one he always sought.

"How was the job interview?" I asked as he started his vehicle and backed out of my driveway.

"Good, I knew I'd get it. All the guys are pretty tight, so it was just kinda a formality. Five guys own the company. I only know a few of them from high school."

"Excited?"

"It'll be nice to have something to keep me busy. What about you? Did you send the final design to your client?"

"Yes, but I'm waiting for the notes of death on it. He hasn't been happy with any of them. Part of me thinks he just doesn't like me working on his project."

"I'm sure that's not true, but if it is, then he's an asshole."

"He is, and you can tell the bias by the way he treats everyone else." I didn't want to talk about the biggest problem with my job. "This is our first date…I don't want to talk about work. So where are you taking me?"

"And I think I've said before it was a surprise."

When he glanced at me, I pouted and batted my lashes.

"As cute as you are, you're going to learn patience."

I rolled my eyes and crossed my arms.

"You're going to get a spanking when we get home."

The warning in his voice was all promise, and my body responded to it. I don't know why I felt more like myself since he returned. Maybe more the person I was supposed to be, yet I was still unsure if it would last. I hated thinking Bern was just having fun with me. The part of my brain that I'd tried to turn off was formulating what a life with Bern would be like. Coming home after a shitty day to curl up on his lap. Having him cuddle me at night. Brutally fuck me as he claimed me as his boy.

It was so odd to relax with a sense of contentment at the possibilities. We pulled into a parking lot, and only a few vehicles littered the space. He made no move to get out, and I turned my head to find him watching me. I gasped as his strong hand gripped my thigh and tucked his thick fingers between my legs. Every muscle tensed as he forced my legs apart with a jerk, and he was rubbing my dick through my slacks.

As he worked my length, he leaned over the console, and his free hand cupped my face. He placed his lips against mine. "After our date, Daddy wants to take his boy home to play with him. Do you want that?"

I could only hum a yes as I rode the cup of his palm. Last night, while we'd kissed and made out before he'd gone home to his own bed, he hadn't touched me like this. The sun hadn't gone down completely, so I was nervous someone would see, but he didn't seem to have the same reservations.

"Does my boy like when Daddy touches him?"

"Yes. But I shouldn't."

I couldn't stop myself from humping into his hand and gripping his wrist with both hands.

I slammed my eyes closed as I tried to calm down, forcing my hips to still. His breath fanned the side of my neck, and his lips barely brushed my skin.

"Why shouldn't you enjoy when your Daddy touches you? Why do you want to deny yourself the one thing you've always desired?"

He placed the softest kisses to my pulse, and that sent an arc of pleasure through me that even his hand massaging my cock couldn't produce. I loved it when he touched me. He did it all the time, and I felt wanted—desired. I raised my arm to stroke his bearded cheek and moaned as his hand left my crotch to grip the side of my neck, and he bit my throat.

"Answer me, boy."

"I'm scared that this is just a dream and I'll wake up. Embarrassed when I try to look at the real you."

"Baby boy, this is real. Less than a week and I'm already addicted to touching you...kissing you. The sexy way you whimper *Daddy* all needy. You want your Daddy's cock. Want Daddy to hurt you when he fucks you so you feel owned."

"Daddy."

His grip on me became painful as he found my mouth and kissed me—hard. Pushing my head back into the headrest under the punishing pressure and just as I was ready to beg him to take me home, he left me wanting.

"Behave while we have dinner, and I will give you everything you need when we get home."

We made our way inside, and I was in a haze, my face flamed as he pulled out my chair. I loved the gentlemanly actions. It was perfectly natural and felt effortless, not as if he were acting. Insecurity hit me for a moment when the server came to the table. Lean and perfect, the interest in his pretty green eyes apparent. But when I glanced at Bern, I found him staring right at me—his sexy smirk made promises I was sure he was going to keep.

"What did you want, baby?"

I stuttered out my drink order as he winked at me, and then ordered a soda.

When the server left the table, I smiled at him. "You could've had a drink."

"No, you enjoy yourself. I have to make sure you get home safely."

I knew my expression looked silly as hell, but he just made me smile.

"It's all overwhelming."

"What is?" He slid his hand across the table to lace his fingers with mine.

"You."

"I don't see a reason to hide my feelings for you. You'll just have to get used to it."

"Lawrence didn't touch me in public or let people know we were together. He'd stopped inviting me to work events so he didn't have to introduce his husband."

"His loss because I want to do nothing more than show you off. Everyone will know you're mine."

Mine. That word played on repeat in my brain throughout dinner and conversation. My nerves increased as the full extent of what the night meant. I'd only been with one person in my life, and over the years, he'd found me lacking. What would Bern think? Would he find me lacking for my lack of experience? I'd always believed that the man I fell in love with would be the last. And I was finally beginning to look forward to starting over with Bern. He embraced all the parts of me that I'd torn myself down about and his desires matched mine. He wanted nothing more than to be my Daddy and take care of me as his boy. My insecurities in the face of the newness were riding me hard, and as much as I tried to push them to the back of my mind, I was trapped in the old cycle of the neglected and unwanted husband. I wanted my Daddy to keep me, and he promised me that he wanted nothing other than to be with me. He'd waited years for me and was going nowhere. And I hope he held on tight because I needed his strength and care. I'd existed a lifetime for it.

8

BERN

Through dinner and the ride home, all I could think about was taking my boy in hand. I knew no one had treated him the way he deserved, and I needed to make sure he knew that I wanted him in every way. And that meant in my life and bed. As much as it pained me that he wasn't all the way convinced what was happening between us was real, I had all the time to prove it to him.

The fact he still bore some shame from his desire to be a Daddy's boy was going to make this an uphill battle, but I hadn't waited as many years as I had to give up. I had decades of damage to erase from Lawrence's actions. When Dad had gone to the party the bastard invited him to, he bragged about all the good things he had in life now that he was single. Dad had told me he'd made his excuses and left early because he couldn't take the attitude of his former friend. The utter disrespect for Devon was clear in the way the bastard had spoken about his ex-husband. Dad had barely talked me out of making a visit to his new house.

But tonight wasn't about Lawrence—it was about showing Devon he was mine.

We stepped up onto his porch, and I took the keys from his hand as I pressed fully to his back. I loved how he gripped my thighs as if to ground himself. I longed to be the one he came to for his comfort. I unlocked the door, opened it, and used my body to nudge him inside.

"Turn around," I ordered as I slowly closed the door until the lock clicked. "Take three steps backward." Again, he obeyed and my already thickening cock hardened further. I didn't think to hide it as I adjusted myself into a more comfortable position. With my total focus on him, I tossed his keys and the contents of my own pockets into the bowl beside the door. I removed my jacket slowly and hung it up, I felt his gaze on me and unbuttoned my cuffs and rolled them over my forearms. Turning my head slightly, I waited until he looked at me.

“Strip.”

“What?”

I stood my ground. “We’re going to establish some rules over the course of tonight, and one of those is, you will always be naked when Daddy is around. Now, I won’t punish you this first time, but you will follow my rules from here forward.”

His face turned the brightest red. While I'd stripped and bathed him already, being nude with me was still new, but it was better to take care of ridding him of his insecurities from minute one. He was trembling so badly I had to wait long moments for him to unbutton his shirt and the cuffs. He exposed pale, flawless skin as he removed it. He had the cutest little belly. As he dropped the first item of clothing, he moved onto his pants and paused.

“Boy, Daddy likes what he sees. Continue.” He cast me a shy glance, and after what seemed like forever, he stood bare in front of me. “Go bend over the back of the couch, spread your cheeks for me.”

He was barely holding himself together, and I wasn't far behind. My dream come true was here, and if I touched him right now, I'd fuck him. Despite our phone sex experience, I knew he might not be ready to move to sex yet. Yet, I wanted to play with him anyway.

I rumbled deep in my chest as he positioned himself just as I ordered. His hole exposed for me. I wanted to eat my boy's ass until he was begging and whimpering, grinding on my tongue. The urge was strong, but I ignored it.

I approached and stopped behind him. "It's time Daddy lets you play with your new toys." I opened the box of prepared toys and lube. I picked up the plug. It was big enough to make my boy feel full and stretched, but he'd still feel the burn of my cock sinking into him for the first time. But I needed to remember that tonight wasn't about me. I slicked it, then rested my left hand on the small of his back.

He arched as just the tapered tip entered him. "Does my boy like his ass fucked?"

"Yes, Daddy." His voice broke over my title.

I steadily pushed the toy inside, watching the way his rim gripped the surface and he shook so forcefully I had to hold him down. His skin became slick with sweat. He pulled his cheeks farther apart as his ass closed around the thickest point, and it sunk all the way in. I placed my hand under him to spread over his chest and helped him straighten. His pretty pink cock was hard and begging for his Daddy's attention.

"Are you going to thank Daddy for your present?"

I saw his indecision, but then he lifted onto his toes and kissed my cheek.

"Don't you want to give Daddy a big boy kiss?"

He nodded and gave me a shy glance from under his long lashes. His hands spreading over my chest was heaven and hell, but the almost innocent kiss came close to my undoing.

His tongue tentatively teased the seam of my lips, and I captured his mouth with a savage need to possess him. He was rubbing his cock against my thigh, and I popped his ass cheek in a warning.

"You don't get to rub on Daddy unless he gives you permission."

"Sorry, Daddy."

"It's okay. If you're good while Daddy plays with you, then I'll let you suck Daddy's cock. Would you like that?"

"Very much."

I took his hand and led him around the couch. When I sat down, I tugged him until he sat heavily on my thigh.

"Before we start, Daddy is going to give you a word to use. If you get uncomfortable or Daddy hurts you, you say it, and all play ends. Do you understand?" I wanted to push his limits of what he'd done before, but I also wanted him to have the option of backing out if I made him uncomfortable or did something he didn't like. Whatever happened between us was consensual, and if I didn't make him feel good, then I'd failed at my job as his Daddy.

"Yes, Daddy."

"Your safe word is Purple." He repeated it when I asked him to, then I raised my right hand and stroked just the tips of my fingers down his chest. Over the curve of his cute belly, and just when I reached his cock, I stopped. He let out the sweetest whine. "You're beautiful. Soft and so shy."

He lowered his chin to his chest and hid his face from me. That didn't conceal the pretty blush that stained his face. For a man of his age, I found his sweetness arousing. I wanted to give him the experiences he'd only ever dreamed of. No one had ever given him the reality of being the submissive boy he longed to be. I wanted to be the Daddy he'd waited so long for, and I refused to fail him.

"You never have to worry that I'll hurt you."

"I know. I'm not afraid of you."

I stroked the gentle lines of his body with just the tips of my fingers. Light enough to simply tease and his response was what I'd anticipated. The smallest touch made him shake on my lap. His breaths were shuddering from between his perfect lips.

"Do you touch yourself thinking about Daddy?" I asked him as I drew my gaze down his body to his hard cock that was leaving a wet spot on my shirt. I brutally fisted my hand in his hair and jerked his head back. His heavy-lidded eyes met mine. Everything he felt and hoped to hide was right there on display for me. He'd allow me to do whatever I wanted as long as I continued to love on him.

"Yes, Daddy. It feels better when I think about you."

"You shouldn't touch yourself when Daddy can't see." I slowly brought his mouth to mine with his hair still wrapped around my fist. I kept our lips apart. I wanted him to ask me for what he wanted and to understand that I was in charge. My boy would always listen, but soon he'd have to learn to take my punishments too.

"I-I'm sorry."

"Daddy made you a list of rules. And as we get to know each other, discuss our expectations and your limits, we'll add to it." I removed the folded sheet of paper from my pocket where I'd placed it when I'd gotten ready earlier and handed it to him. "Read your rules, boy."

"Per Daddy these rules may be amended at any time. Rule one...I will trust Daddy to know what is best for me." He glanced shyly at me, and I tapped the paper to keep him reading. "Rule two...I will always be ready to please Daddy with my mouth or ass. Rule three...I will always be naked in our home. Rule four...Daddy will punish me if I disobey rules, put myself in danger, or lie to Daddy. Rule five...rewards will be earned and taken away depending on Daddy's discretion."

I watched him as he read every line slowly and deferring to me with a pause as he studied me. I played with his pretty dick, distracting him as he recited the rules and making him stutter. The head of his cock was shining with pre-cum. When he turned to the second page, which was just a single piece of paper that showed him my negative results for STDs and HIV. During some of our conversations, he'd told me his fears of Lawrence cheating on him and how he'd gone through monthly tests since his divorce—even though he'd taken the same ones during his yearly physicals. The last ten years of his marriage he'd feared his husband's disinterest was due to fucking around, so he'd thought better to be safe than sorry.

"I wanted you to know that you're always safe with me and you're it for me. When I take you, I don't want any barriers between us, but when that happens, it's your choice. Even now, you're naked on my lap, plug in, yet sex doesn't have to happen anytime soon."

"You'd wait?"

"I've waited for you for thirteen years. I know you're still unsure"—he opened his mouth to protest, and I cut him off with a quick kiss—"Don't lie to me, baby boy. You seeing me as a grown man is still new, and I know you're still frightened to take me seriously. I can only promise that I'll never lie to you."

"Okay."

"Since it's our first night of playtime, you can have anything you want."

"Anything, Daddy?"

"I'm yours."

I kissed his eyes closed as I listened to his soft sob, and when he slipped from my lap, I resisted the urge to keep him close. His hands had a fine tremor as he knelt between my legs and worked my shirt buttons free. When we'd slept together, I'd kept my clothes on to control myself. When he reached my waistband, I leaned forward and shrugged my shirt off. I groaned and let my head fall back as he combed his fingers through the thick hair on my stomach and chest. I gripped his sides just under his armpits as his soft palms dragged over my nipples.

"May I, Daddy?" he asked as he lifted one of my hands to wrap around the back of his neck.

I jerked him forward, and he nuzzled my hairy skin. He moaned, and I felt him inhale.

"You smell so good, Daddy."

I rubbed his head as he drifted south, and I felt him working my belt loose—the button and zipper undone. He buried his face against my cotton covered groin. My boy whimpered and moaned. I allowed him to tug my pants and boxer briefs to the middle of my hairy thighs.

I cursed as he laid his head on my thigh and wrapped his hand around the base of my cock, then he took a few inches into his mouth. My boy was sucking my cock like he would his thumb to go to sleep. I could just see him working his little cock. I kept my hips still, and his cheek stroked over my leg as he laid there quietly jerking off. The only sounds were his heavy breathing and soft suckling sounds.

"So pretty." My voice was gruffer as I traced the corner of his mouth that was stretched around the girth of my dick. Sweat was beading in my body hair as my pleasure increased witnessing his contentment at just suckling me and playing with himself. My balls ached with the need to come, but the more I denied myself and focused on his comfort, the less I wanted to get off.

"Daddy loves when his little boy sucks his cock." My heart pounded an almost painful rhythm in my chest. He wasn't drawing hard or taking more than those few inches. I felt the curl of his tongue, the ridged texture of the roof of his mouth. As turned on as I was, as much as I wanted to come, I could sense a calmness in him. I grunted as he released me with a soft pop.

"Is that how you want Daddy to put you to bed every night?"

"Yes, Daddy. You feel better than when I suck my thumb."

"You're Daddy's good little boy." I helped him onto the couch, and he reached for me as I got up.

I stood before him and stripped. I watched him as I exposed every inch of my body for him. I couldn't miss the way he swallowed hard and licked his lips as I picked up the lube, slicking my cock with a few rough strokes. I sat back down as I turned on the TV, and found a cartoon channel for him, and pushed his legs open to remove his plug. "Sit on Daddy's lap and watch your cartoons." He started to sit on my thigh, and I shifted him until he could slide down my cock.

"Daddy won't hurt his boy. He knows you've been thinking about playing with it." I groaned long and deep as his hole wrapped around my length. He was so tight he was strangling my cock with his rim. "Goddamn, boy." I held his cheeks apart as his ass met my groin, and I watched him take every thick inch. My hands moved to his hips, and they were so big my fingertips met the trimmed curls at the base of his dick. "Get comfortable, baby."

We both shook as his back met my chest, and I caressed him as we pretended to watch TV. His cheek was pressed to mine, and every once in a while, I turned to kiss his cheek—the corner of his mouth. I felt the subtle shift of his hips as I felt him flexing his ass around where I was buried deep. We were teasing each other. It was taking everything in me to keep control, but after years, I finally felt like I was where I belonged. While I wanted to fuck him right now, I wanted the intimacy more.

"Daddy?"

"Yes, baby."

"Do I feel good?" he asked as he started to stroke his slim length.

"You feel so good. Hot and tight."

"Daddy, can I ask you something?"

I kissed his cheek and then buried my face against his throat. "You can ask me anything."

"Will you love me?"

At his shy, teary question, I lifted him off me and scooped him into my arms. "Do you want me to love on you as Daddy or Bern?"

"Both."

I kissed him gentle and slow as I carried him upstairs to the bedroom. I laid him easily on the bed and then stretched out between his slender thighs. I used my hand to hold my length steady as I pushed into him. I tasted his pretty whine as I seated myself fully. I curled my arms beneath him, grabbed his shoulders as I started to move. Tender, shallow strokes as he touched me with tentative hands.

"I've loved you for so long, baby. Always you." The achingly slow pace didn't change as I placed the softest kisses on his parted lips as we stared into each other's eyes. Our sweaty bodies moved together in a sensuous rhythm with no need to hurry to the finish line.

"I was so ashamed." He sobbed, and I hurt as I watched tears slip from the corners of his eyes, into his tangled hair.

"There's no shame in what we want."

"I want to feel you come in me. Show me you own me."

That's all I needed to hear. I didn't just start pounding him, I worked into a lazily increasing pace until I shoved every screamed grunt from him. The teasing went on too long, I was so close, but I made sure to rub his hard dick between our bellies as I fucked into him with brutal snaps of my hips.

"Squeeze me, work for your reward, boy."

His thighs parted wider and his hips tilted, and his eyes went wide as his lips parted on a silent scream.

A squeaked *hurt me, Daddy* past his lips, and I surged upward, sitting back on my heels as I worked his little cock in my fist as I watched my cock abuse his swollen hole. The second I felt his seed over my hand, I slammed into him hard enough to push his head into the pillows and filled him with every drop of cum. The cut of my abs was drawn in tighter as I jerked.

"Fuck, boy, take it," I ordered him as I started fucking him again, seeing my cum and slick covered cock appear and disappear until I collapsed on top of him. My lips were on his as I kissed and calmed him, as his much smaller body shook beneath mine. "You'll never get away from me now. You feel my ownership? My fat cock and cum deep inside you. Always mine."

Long minutes later, I eased from him and carried him to the bathroom to shower us to prepare for bed. He didn't move away from me as I stroked my hands over him. I chuckled as he flinched as I found a ticklish spot. I drew his arms from around my neck so I could wash his front, then get us out of the stall. I didn't hesitate to pick him back up to carry him to bed, stretching out beside him as we softly talked until I saw his eyes close.

I caressed his cheek with the backs of my fingers as his breathing evened out, and I cuddled him tight to me. I drifted off to sleep content for the first time in my life.

9

DEVON

I smiled all through my first day back to work after my weekend spent with Daddy Bern. He was so sexual I thought it would be non-stop fucking after he took me, but last night I'd fallen asleep sucking his cock as he stroked my hair. Then I'd awakened this morning with his body blanketing mine, and he'd fucked me until I came on the sheets beneath me. He was still hard because he hadn't found release, but he'd gotten me ready for work, bathed, dressed, and breakfast. A kiss at the door as he told me to have a good day at work.

After our date on Saturday night, I'd never experienced that level of intimacy. We watched TV with me on his cock, just touching and kissing, and he never seemed in a hurry to climax. He sent me messages throughout the day to check on me. To make sure I wasn't too sore or had I had a snack or meal yet. I think some might think that was stifling, but I loved it. It was even better when I received flowers and dessert mid-afternoon. I fingered the velvety petals as I waited for my day to end.

"Well, well, well, someone is dating again?"

Tiffany was one of the newest architects that I'd kind of became friendly with, in the past year. I jerked my head up and tried to rid my mouth of the silly grin. Then my phone chimed, and I checked it to find a shirtless and sweaty Daddy smirking at me, the caption read: *I'll be home at 5. Remember the rules.*

"Oh, you gotta let me see what—"

I tried to hide my phone before Tiff got a peek and was too late. I was too shocked at seeing my man telling me to be naked when he got home.

"Holy shit, is he yours?"

"Yes, but it's kinda new. He just moved home after being gone for several years." I didn't mention he was my best friend's son.

"You are one lucky man. You have to invite me and my husband over for dinner. I have to see that man in person."

"I'll talk to him when I get home."

"That man has more abs than is humanly possible."

I locked my phone because I didn't like her drooling over my Daddy.

"I'd be jealous, too. It's good to see you happy."

I felt silly when she called me on my jealousy. Never once during my marriage had I felt possessive, but suddenly I didn't want to share. It was still new, and I was processing that the younger man wanted me for his boy.

"I don't think I've seen you genuinely smile at work in a long time. We should have drinks even if you don't want me drooling over your man."

"I'd actually like that. Since the divorce, I haven't been out much until Bern."

"Time to move on, to be honest, the few times I met Lawrence, I wasn't a fan."

I found that surprising because everyone seemed to love Lawrence. He was outgoing and fun, handsome. The perfect manipulator and I hadn't seen the extent of it until the relationship was all over. Sometimes I wondered how much I'd unconsciously forgiven in order to keep my marriage—to not be alone.

"He just seemed a bit stuck up."

"I didn't realize it before."

"My first husband was the same way. I didn't realize the toxic environment until I met my current husband. To be honest, I almost turned him down for a date because I didn't believe he was actually…nice."

"He's a lot younger than me."

"Um, flowers, special afternoon treat, and shirtless selfies…I don't think he has an issue."

I turned my head to cover another stupid grin.

"And, honey, that smile says you don't care either. I'll leave you to work and remember, drinks after work one night if you can pull yourself away from your sexy ginger."

"I'll talk to Bern about that dinner."

"Sounds good, honey. Just keep smiling like that."

I kept my gaze on her until she disappeared and then decided to break off early to make dinner before he got home. I bit off a groan of disgust as Mr. Hatcher, my boss, entered my office with that look on his face thinking I was going to put in extra time.

"Devon, I'm going to need you to stay over, I received some—"

"The design is final, and if he has another complaint, you can assign him to another architect. I've put up with his passive-aggressive bullshit for over a month. I'm done. My boyfriend is going to be home at five, and we're having dinner."

"Devon, he doesn't want to work with anyone else, he just has a few more—"

"Have you viewed the designs? The building is a

monstrosity that will be a blight in that neighborhood, and he only wants bigger and bigger. If you can't deal with that, I can give my resignation." I packed the rest of my stuff in my messenger bag and slung the strap over my shoulder. "I've bitten my tongue long enough about his obvious bias toward me. Either he's a bigot or just an asshole. Now, good night, Mr. Hatcher."

"Devon, please, there's no need—" I rolled my eyes as I stepped around him and walked out into the outer office. "Please, there's no need for you to, I'll have it taken, Devon, just a minute—"

I entered the elevator and turned to face him with a smile. "Goodnight, Mr. Hatcher." I raised my hand and wiggled my fingers in a goodbye motion, then the door closed.

I chuckled to myself all the way down to the lobby and then left the building feeling lighter. I wasn't going to put up with any more disrespect. I didn't deserve it, and I'd kept my mouth shut for too long. It was time I did what made me happy, and that was going home to wait for Daddy.

I HEARD THE FRONT DOOR OPEN, AND I KEPT mashing the potatoes. The closer his heavy steps got, the more I tensed with excitement at him being home. His growl echoed seconds before I was in his arms.

"Now, this is what your Daddy wants to see when I get home."

I lifted my shoulder to keep him from tickling my neck with his beard. I inhaled the scent of sweat and man as he pressed fully to my back. I raised my right hand to rub his cheek as he seemed to try to squeeze the life out of me.

"Fuck, you always feel good."

I moaned as his left hand cupped my dick through the

apron I wore. I wasn't using a stove naked. I yelped as he spun me and I found myself sitting on the counter, my thighs pushed wide by his hips. He was breathing roughly against my mouth. I fisted my hands in the sides of his damp shirt.

"I missed my boy today."

"I missed you too, Daddy," I whispered the last word and was rewarded with a deep kiss.

"Say it again, boy," he demanded as he removed the apron and dropped it to the floor.

"Daddy." I went from making dinner to too turned on to think within seconds.

"Were you a good boy today?"

"I like to think so. A friend from work asked if I wanted to have drinks one night after work."

"And?"

I almost grinned at the dangerous edge to his voice because I hadn't mentioned if the friend was male or female.

"My possessive Daddy. I told her I had to talk to you. She wants to have dinner so she can see my man in person."

"I'd love to have dinner with your friends." He stroked the sides of my thighs as he seemed to study me as if he were looking for something. "Unless you want to maybe keep me hidden."

"Of course not, Bern, the age difference only bothered me for a bit because of my need for a Daddy and I thought I was too old for that. I wouldn't hide you for anything. She may be a little jealous about my hot ginger boyfriend."

"Was she?"

I hummed an affirmative as I tipped my head so he could nip at the side of my throat. I combed my fingers through his hair and held him in place as I felt the sting as he sucked at my pulse.

"Some of the guys are getting together Friday night, them and their significant others. I want to take my boy with me."

"You want me to go out with you and your friends?"

"I want to show you off. I told them I'd have the hottest person on my arm."

"Who are you taking? Someone young and cute?" I yelled as he smacked my thigh.

"You want to ask me that again? You haven't been put over my knee yet."

"You wouldn't," I said and realized that was the wrong reply.

He backed up and pulled out one of the kitchen chairs. He sat down and patted his thighs.

"Lie right here…now."

I wanted to protest, but the look in his eyes made me roll my lips between my teeth. I lowered my feet to the floor and approached slowly, my stomach twisted with knots. I laid myself across his lap, and his right arm became a brace across my lower back.

"You may have been joking, but I need you to understand that I only do this to correct your thinking. You're more to me than some meaningless fuck, you're mine, and I adore every inch of you."

His voice was hard, and the first strike had me wiggling to get away. It wasn't a sensual spanking—this was punishment. I may have been joking when I asked if he was taking someone else, but my distorted thinking made me second guess if I wanted to meet his friends and have them look at me—wonder what Daddy saw in me.

"You're beautiful and perfect to me."

Another landed, and fire spread across my ass cheeks. It hurt, but even as Daddy corrected me, his voice softened.

"I have loved you for years. I don't want anyone else."

The third, fourth, and fifth ones had my hips arching as the pain intensified. Tears filled my eyes as he spanked me and listed all the things that he loved about me. Told me that

I was his boy and he was a lucky Daddy for having me. Something inside me broke, and I buried my face in my hands. I was lifted to curl up on his lap. He stroked my back, kissed my brow, and I felt very much outside myself. He pulled my hands away from my face, and with gentle fingertips, he lifted my gaze to his.

"Lawrence treated you as if you were a burden and undesirable, you are neither of those things to me. I don't want to hurt you, but I need you to get out of the mindset that exists from his actions. I need you to understand that Daddy loves you, always has, and one day I hope you love me too. Until then, I will love and care for you, correct you when needed. You won't put yourself down in my presence. Do you understand?"

"Yes, Daddy. Can you just hold me?"

"For however long you need me too. Did you want to lie down with Daddy for a short nap?"

I couldn't speak as the lump in my throat seemed to get bigger so I nodded and he easily stood with me cradled in his arms. I hugged him and pressed my face to his throat as he carried me through the house and up to the bedroom. My ass was sore, and the burn was almost too much. He stretched out on the bed, pulling a throw blanket over me. I was suddenly tired, and my mind kept going back to all the things I'd learned in my marriage. How much of it left a mental scar? Had I started to see myself as Lawrence had and take the blame for the divorce?

"Just close your eyes, boy, Daddy will hold you. And when you wake up, I'll give you a nice long bath and feed you."

I felt more than heard his chuckle as I crawled on top of him, pushing his shirt up until I could nuzzle hairy skin and he readjusted the blanket. He soothingly stroked his rough hands up and down my back as I felt my lids grow heavy. I'd never grow tired of how he made me feel safe and loved. At almost fifty, I just realized how lonely my life was up until him. Even when he was just my best friend's kid, looking back, he did special things that I'd taken for granted. A book I mentioned I wanted to read that I didn't think anyone was paying attention to me when I'd said it. Small pieces here and there that I'd stared at for a second longer than normal in the store. Each one found its way to me for birthdays or holidays—sometimes he'd just drop something off and leave. I needed to do better. I wasn't the man I was a year ago, and I needed to learn to move forward.

10

BERN

I hated punishing him, but I'd only done it because he needed it. Three days later, I was still agonizing over the fact I hurt him, but I couldn't let him make jokes about himself. He might think it was the thing to say, brush off his insecurities as a non-issue. That wasn't what it was at all. He'd only accepted my claim a few weeks earlier, and we had a long way to go for me to get Lawrence's poison out of his mind.

"That is not the look of a man in love."

I turned my head to find my dad studying me from where he stood in the kitchen doorway. Devon was having drinks with his friend Tiffany from work, and I didn't want to stay in that house without him.

"I had to punish him."

"Your mother always hated when she had to correct me. She always wanted to be the loving and caring Domme. I understood why she did it, and I'm sure he knows too."

"Doesn't make it right. I told him I wanted him to go with me to hang out with the guys I work with. He made a joke about taking someone younger and cute."

"Bern, he's insecure, and you know why, but you can't let him get away with denigrating himself. He needs to learn his worth, and sometimes, you need to take him in hand."

"I know, but it was his first punishment."

"Did you gently bring him down?"

"Yes, we took a nap, then I gave him a bath."

"Your mom would be so proud of you."

I grinned as he walked behind me and only paused long enough to drop a kiss on the top of my head. I remember when I was little and something was bothering me, he'd do the same. My life had always been filled with love. Dad had always made sure I was safe and happy. I wondered what life would've been like if my mother had survived. He always assured me she would've felt pride in the boy I was and the man I became. I didn't remember her. The only memories I had were the stories he told me and the videos that she'd left behind.

"Dad, do you have the videos Mom left for me?"

"Yes, I had them converted to disks a few years ago." He disappeared, and I almost yelled at him that he didn't have to get them now, but he was back within minutes with a stack of disks.

She'd left three sets, one for Dad, one for us and the last set just for me. Dad had never watched mine, and his were private.

"Do you still watch yours?"

"Yes."

I didn't ask him to explain. They were words special to him, and I wondered if she'd left him with videos to help him find his center long after she was gone.

"Maybe you should go check those out. There's a few new ones in there."

"New?"

"Yes, I thought about sending them to you while you were

away, but when you were deployed and all that, I didn't think whatever advice she gave you you'd want to share with others. They were in her safety deposit box, and there's some she left for after you found your person."

"You didn't tell me."

"You've been distracted with claiming your boy. Why don't you go next door and watch them alone?"

I held them tightly until the edges of the cases cut into my hands, and I stood. I dropped my left hand from the bundle and wrapped my arm around him.

"Thank you."

"Your mom loved you from the moment she knew she was pregnant. Said you were the greatest gift next to my trust that she'd ever received. Go spend some time with your mom."

I reluctantly released him and quickly headed back to Devon's. As I was standing in front of the TV, I flipped through until I found the new ones, and chose the one that was labeled, *When you find your one.* I put the disk into the DVD player and backed up until I fell onto the couch. I fumbled the remote as I took deep breaths and tried to find my calm before pressing play.

A beautiful face with a fall of bright red curls stared at me. Every video was the same, she looked so serene, even knowing that her time was limited.

"Hi, Bern. Well, this is a special video. I had Murray save it until just this moment. If you're like me"—she took a deep breath—*"you saw your one, and nothing would stop you from having them. I don't know if you grew up to be gay or straight, whether you just love the person, but if you've met them, I'm so happy for you."*

I saw the tears fill her eyes as if she was mourning the fact that she wouldn't be here to meet the person I was going to make mine.

"I wish I could be there when you made your vows. I know your

dad. I know I left you in the best hands. You'll know what true love is. I know you're probably well past the sex talk stage and I won't embarrass you by giving you advice on how to please your person. I'm here to tell you how to care for your person. To make sure you instill peace in your person.

"Let me start by saying, when I met Murray, I could see the shadows in his eyes. He didn't understand how deeply I would come to love him. I watched as he tore himself down and tried to drive me away. Sometimes just telling someone how much you love them doesn't get the point across. It's in how you show them, son. It's the memories you leave behind for them. I won't go into details, but years of videos I've been trying to talk your dad into finding love, but our love was perfect in his eyes. I so wish—" Her voice broke.

Tears filled my eyes as I watched her unashamedly cry as she imagined what leaving her husband behind would do. I just stared at the screen, and I could see all the pain and regret, the anger for her body failing her.

"I so wish that I had a lifetime with him. But in the short time we had together, I know I showed him the love he deserved and that he shouldn't settle for less. And I know I left him in your capable hands. Even as a baby, I could see the calm you had—the empathy. I know your person is incredibly lucky to have you. I'm sure your dad explained what our relationship was like and I don't know if you grew up to be a Dom or not, but it doesn't change the fact that there's things that they're going to need."

I jumped as I felt arms wrap around me, and I glanced over my shoulder to see Devon sitting on the back of the couch. I leaned back between his legs and hit pause. I rested my head on his stomach as he draped his arms over my shoulders.

"She was so beautiful and the harder she fought, the more I was in awe of her."

"I miss her. They say you don't miss what you never had, but I always had her. She made hundreds of videos, some personal for me and Dad, then ones for us to watch together."

"Do you want to be left alone with her?"

"No, you might like this one."

"Your person? I came in a few minutes ago, but if this is something for the two of you, I don't want to intrude."

"Please stay." I tipped my head to get a kiss then wrapped my hand around his arms where he was hugging me. I hit play. I stroked his skin through the linen of his dress shirt.

"*Being in love isn't something we can take lightly. We can't love pieces of a person. You have to accept all their parts, the pretty and the ugly. Your person may come with previous heartaches. Abuse. Traumas that you won't understand, but we love them in such a way that we foster peace and self-worth. Your love isn't enough to repair the damage. Love is merely a band-aid. We have to listen to them. Hear what they say even when they don't want to share everything. Build them up so that they stand beside you knowing that you'll always be there no matter how they stumble.*

"*You correct the damage made. They are a secondhand gift, one that in some cases needs some TLC. But they shine no less bright because they come with a few scars. You love them past that which tried to destroy them.*"

His arms tightened a fraction around me, and I brushed a kiss to his wrist. I savored his warmth and weight. "I always wanted to be for you what Mom was for Dad. I'm scared that I won't do it right."

I let him take the remote, and he paused it. I stared right into my mom's beautiful eyes. Eyes that were exactly like mine. I could see her delicate features in the more masculine and harsher angles of mine. The shape of her mouth. The curl of her hair. That lopsided smile that Dad always said reminded him of her.

"There's no right or wrong here. You've become the man I dreamed of that would've claimed me. We're new. We still have some obstacles to work through. She would've been so proud of you, Bern."

"I hope so. I see Dad, and decades later, the love in his eyes when he talks about Mom is no less bright."

"Let's finish spending time with your mom. I think you need it."

I tugged on his hand until he moved around to curl up on my lap, and he wiggled to get comfortable. I held him close as he pushed play, and we watched the video in silence, sharing kisses and touches. Us just being together with no need to fill the silence beyond the sound of my mom's voice instructing me on how to take care of Devon. And I knew in my heart she would've been ecstatic he was my one.

11

DEVON

I leaned into Bern as Tiff told an embarrassing story about her husband and I laughed louder at the big, scary man's bright red blush. My legs were draped over Daddy's as he held them in place. I couldn't get any closer unless I sat on his lap. He'd been extra cuddly the last few weeks since we'd watched his mom's video. We'd gone for drinks and dinner with his friends from work, and finally, we'd gotten a date finalized to have dinner with Tiff and Ted. The pretty petite woman with her demure clothes hadn't led me to see her married to a huge, tattooed biker with a shaved head, but Ted gave his wife the sweetest looks.

I was having wine with Tiff, as Ted and Bern stuck to non-alcoholic options. We'd arrived two hours ago and still hadn't ordered food, except for appetizers. I couldn't remember the last time I went out on a double date. Hell, I couldn't remember my last date before Bern.

"So, since I embarrassed my husband"—she raised her hand and affectionately tugged his long goatee—"how did you two meet? All Devon told me was that you'd been away for a while."

I held my breath and let him answer.

"It all started when I was fifteen, and I developed a hatred for his husband having what I wanted. And since I couldn't have him"—Bern turned to stare at me with an adoring expression as he stroked the side of my thigh—"I went as far away for college as I could and then enlisted in the Marines. Dad sent me an email a year ago and told me he was free, and I came home when my enlistment was up."

"You waited all those years?"

"Yes, I was probably an annoying teenager with my unrequited love. I got home as soon as I could so no one else would snatch him up before me, but I didn't have to worry too much. I had my dad keeping an eye on my boy. I don't think I gave him much choice."

"I was a little confused, but I quickly smartened up."

"I wasn't going to give up. I've been dreaming and preparing for six years since the last time I saw you."

"So your dad was in on it? Tiff's old man pulled a gun on me when I knocked on the door our first date. Her ex was an asshole. I didn't blame him for being skeptical about me."

Tiff rubbed his chest and leaned into him, his arm automatically going around her. I wondered if I looked as content as she did with her husband?

"His original plan was to hook me up with his dad, who's my best friend."

"The idea didn't last long."

The server approached the table and waited for all of us to look at her. "Are y'all ready to order or another round of drinks?"

"Order, baby," Bern said.

I scanned the menu one more time to see if I still wanted the same thing. I just ordered a salad, next was Tiff and then Bern and Ted. Another round of drinks was ordered, and it would be my last. While I enjoyed the occasional beer, I wasn't much of a drinker, and I didn't want to be asleep before we even got home.

After the server left, we went back to talking and only pausing when drinks arrived.

"Devon, isn't this a surprise."

I tensed at the sound of Lawrence's voice for the first time in almost a year. He hadn't made contact since the divorce was finalized. I tried to remove my legs from Bern's lap, and he gave my thigh a punishing squeeze. He brought his left arm across and pinched my chin, bringing my eyes to his. He leaned forward and pressed his lips to my ear.

"Boy, you don't hide you're mine. Do you understand me?"

I whispered *yes, Daddy* low enough for only him to hear.

"Good boy." He turned my head enough to give me a kiss, and I felt his smile.

Just like that, I was calm. Bern didn't hide his displays of affection or that I was his, and he wanted to make sure I showed everyone he was mine too. Wherever we went, he laced our fingers and kept me close. He was always within arm's length of me so he could touch me whenever he wanted. I was doing better with my insecurity but still lost myself on occasion. He told me he accepted that it would take me a while to start shifting my thinking, but that he would always be there to help.

When he leaned back, I saw the harshness of his features as he turned his attention to Lawrence.

"Lawrence, how are you?"

"I see you're back in town."

"Have been for almost two months. Tiffany, Ted, this is Lawrence."

"We've met briefly at a couple of our work events." I was surprised by Tiff's frosty voice.

Per Lawrence's usual rudeness when he wasn't getting his way, he ignored the other couple. He didn't seem in a hurry to take his narrowed gaze away from Bern and I, and I didn't miss the way he snarled his nose when he saw the way I was sitting.

"Going for a younger man, Devon? Isn't that a little cliched for a middle-aged man?"

"No, you have that backward. You see, when I found out he was free I wasn't letting him get away. I waited a long time for you to get stupid."

I shot a glance at Tiff just in time to see water come out of her nose and Ted was patting her back, wiping her face.

"Why don't you join us for a drink, Lawrence? There's a free chair you can pull up."

Oh, my Daddy was good, his guttural voice all polite. I almost thought Lawrence was going to refuse. Then we had two more people sitting at the table. A beautiful, elegant man with expertly styled hair, maybe in his late thirties.

"I'm Bern, and this is my boyfriend, Devon." Bern offered his hand to the stranger, but his free hand slipped beneath my t-shirt to stroke my lower back in soothing circles. They shared a quick shake, and then Bern was back. He'd shifted and turned slightly until his shoulder rested on my chest, and my chin naturally came to rest on his shoulder. He was putting himself between me and possible threats of any kind.

Lawrence's date was paying a bit too much attention to Bern. I felt a tinge of jealousy, but I trusted Daddy and knew I was it for him. I turned just enough to kiss the side of his neck and inhale his subtle cologne. He was gorgeous, anyone would look, but he nuzzled my smooth cheek with his bearded one. I knew what that beard felt like on every inch of me.

"I'm Jeff, it's a pleasure to meet you. I thought it was just Lawrence and myself tonight."

"I invited him to join us, at least for a drink or two. For old times' sake."

The server came back at that moment with food. Bern set up my food, made sure I had everything I needed before he even looked at his plate. "Please bring him a water with lemon. He's done drinking for tonight."

I smiled as I stared at my plate. He had a way of anticipating my needs before I even knew what I wanted.

"I wish we were at home so I could have my boy sitting on my lap," he whispered in my ear before he checked on everyone else. The meals we shared at home he had me sit on his thigh and fed me each bite. He found enjoyment in taking care of me. Comforting me when I needed it. I even saw the caring in the times he punished me.

He asked the server to bring the new couple drinks and menus.

At first, I felt awkward hearing Lawrence's voice. Yes, I was a bit uncomfortable, but it was seeing my husband who'd asked for a divorce and seemed to go on with his life. I felt my reaction was normal. That didn't mean I didn't feel his glare as it bore into me. We were divorced, and I wasn't doing anything wrong.

"Did you tell Lawrence you got a promotion?" Tiff asked as she delicately picked at her own salad.

"No, Mr. Hatcher said that I showed real assertiveness and exemplary work ethic."

"I still think you should quit and open your own firm, just a small place. Maybe we can find a house where you can have a home office."

"I know, but I cut down on my hours, and I can turn down projects." After I'd stood up for myself, my boss had decided that a pain in the ass client wasn't worth losing me. I'd been there almost since day one. But I appreciated my Daddy's faith in me.

"Whatever makes you happy, baby. Now eat, it's past your dinner time."

"What the fuck is this?" Lawrence demanded. "When did you start fuck—"

"Listen, asshole, I offered you a seat at the table out of politeness, but you will not speak to Devon in that tone. We can continue to purport ourselves like adults with good manners, or you can take your embarrassed date to another table. Show some respect for the gentleman you came with, or you can leave. Your date can stay and enjoy a friendly meal with us."

"Why should I be polite when I just realized you were fucking my husband before you disappeared?"

"Devon showed you respect, and I showed him the same when I didn't put him in that position before I left. You didn't deserve him, and I waited years for him to be free. Now get your ass up before I don't care about making a scene. Devon and I will make sure your date gets home safely."

I held my breath as I waited for Lawrence to lose his mind and start shouting, but in his usual fashion, he left without even giving his date a second glance. I felt sorry for the other man. Jeff was looking everywhere but at us. I'd known Lawrence could be bitchy and cruel, but to leave without offering Jeff a ride home showed shitty behavior.

"I should call a—"

"No, you'll have a nice dinner and drinks, on me, and then we'll get you home. No reason for your night to be ruined." Bern announced and got up, moving the chair Lawrence had used back to the other table.

I observed as Jeff scooted his seat over a bit to get more comfortable and out of the way.

"I could really use a strong drink."

"Then have all the drinks you want, honey, you have a designated driver. We'll take you home or Bern and Devon will. I think you deserve it." Ted waved the server over as she started to pass the table.

I tried not to snort at the look on the elegant man's face by being called honey by a scary biker. Jeff ordered his food and a mixed drink instead of the original wine.

"What is it you do, Jeff?" I asked to include him in the conversation.

"I'm a photographer and journalist. I do a lot of travel articles and the occasional freelance piece."

"I'm sorry for Lawrence, that was rude."

"Devon, don't apologize, it was a blind date. My friends swore they had the nicest guy. To be honest, I'd almost called to cancel, but I don't like doing that last minute even if I've never met the person before. This seems like a better evening. I had an odd feeling since he picked me up."

The rest of the night was very much how it started, laid-back conversation, too much to drink, and when I refused dessert, Bern ordered me my favorite for later. On an unconscious level, I think I'd started comparing Bern and Lawrence's treatment of me. Even in the honeymoon phase of my relationship and marriage to Lawrence, I'd sensed something wasn't right. Bern was respectful of my limits, listened to me complain, offered his opinion, but never guilted me into complying. While the sex was amazing, it was more than that.

I sometimes had a fleeting thought about what would've happened if he'd told me before he left for the Marines. Yet, I could admit I wouldn't have accepted it. Everything happened at the time it's supposed to, and in analyzing Lawrence's role as my husband, after the divorce, I started to realize what I wanted and needed. I gave Bern my weight, and he automatically shifted until he could cuddle me to his side with his arm tightly around me. I just needed to work a bit more on my insecurities. He didn't hesitate to say he loved me, but I had to learn what it was like to truly love in return before I could say it.

12

BERN

"Hey, baby boy, you're home early," I called out as I closed the door behind me. "I thought you had a business dinner." I tossed my phone on the table along with my keys and strode through the house to the kitchen. I had a surprise for my boy. I froze in the doorway as I caught sight of my boy coming toward me. He was naked per my rules, but if it was up to me, he'd be home waiting for me naked every night.

And what I loved the most, was the small smile as he approached. His confidence grew every day, and I was so proud of him. As soon as he was close enough, I grabbed his hips and jerked him against me. I lowered my mouth to his and brought my hands up to sink into his soft hair. A rumbling sound worked its way up from my chest as he shoved his hands under my shirt to get to my hairy stomach and higher to my chest. My boy loved his hairy Daddy.

I reluctantly broke the kiss. "I missed you today, boy."

"I missed you too. Daddy, will you go to my work dinner with me tonight?"

"Do you want me there?"

He nodded as I placed gentle kisses to his lips. I could spend hours just kissing and holding him.

"Then, yes, I'll go. What do I need to wear?"

"I bought you something to wear."

"Baby, you don't have to buy me things."

"I know, but I wanted to. And to be honest, I wanted to see you in a suit."

"Ulterior motives. When do we have to leave?"

"We have to be at the restaurant in a few hours."

"Then, I have time to discuss something with you first." I backed up to the kitchen table, sat down onto a chair, and drew him down onto my lap. "Were you a good boy today?"

"Yes, Daddy."

His shy tone made my cock harden, but we didn't have time for me to take care of my boy as I liked. He liked to be played with and teased—loved on as he deserved. I wanted him constantly, and we were coming up on three months since he agreed to be mine. He'd taken a few business trips, and even though I hated it, I knew since the arrangement changed at work, he loved his job. Video calls and texts throughout the day helped, but a week or two without him hadn't set right with me.

I raised my left hand and stroked down the center of his body, teasing the curve of his belly and cupped his cock. He rolled his hips, and I circled his pretty dick. I slowly jacked his length. I caught his gaze with mine.

"Daddy's boy deserves a reward for being good."

His sexy, breathy moans came faster as he shifted to straddle my thighs with his back to my chest. I played with his right nipple, then the other and bit at his shoulder.

"When we get home from dinner, I'll let you watch TV while you sit on Daddy's cock."

"Th-thank you." He gasped as I wrapped my big hand around the front of his throat. He tipped his head back as I squeezed just enough until his pleasure-induced moans turned to rasps and he fucked my fist. "Daddy, please."

I released the slight pressure as he drew in deep breaths and then did it again. "You like when Daddy controls you. Come for Daddy, boy."

His movements became desperate, and then his seed covered my hand, and I squeezed my thumb and forefinger just under the head, milking every ounce. I didn't stop until he collapsed against my chest, and I raised my hand to his mouth. "Clean up your mess." I spread my hand across his pelvis and worked his ass against my bulge as he sucked and licked my fingers. When he sucked two past his lips, I pushed in deeper until he gagged for me.

I wrapped my arms around him and hugged him tight to me as I pressed my face to his neck. Kissing and inhaling the scent that was all my boy's, I'd never get tired of him being mine.

"Now, I don't want to go to dinner, Daddy."

"Well, you have to, it's for work. I want you to move in with me."

Suddenly he was standing but just as quickly seated himself back on my lap, his inner thighs gripping my hips.

"You want us to live together?"

"Of course, I thought maybe we could look at houses. Something that's just ours. What do you think?" I curled my hands around his sides and drew my thumbs over his soft skin, sinking into his belly I loved so much.

"I'd love that."

"Then we'll call an agent and start looking at places."

He giggled and hugged my neck, kissing all over my face. I chuckled at his excitement. I knew he wasn't ready for the question I really wanted to ask, but one day we'd get to that point. While I wanted my ring on his finger, it wasn't a future requirement. Either way, I was planning to spend the rest of my life with him.

"If that made you happy, what would you say if I reserved us a cabin in the woods for a weekend? That place you always wanted to go."

"On Henderson Lake?"

"Yes."

"You remembered."

I took his face in my hands and swiped away his tears with my thumbs. I hated thinking about Lawrence, but there were so many things my boy wanted to do and felt he couldn't have because of his ex-husband.

"Baby, there's not much I don't remember about you, and I have a list of all the trips you wanted to take and never could. We're going to make them all, but I thought the lake was a good starting point. I took off Friday. We can head up there for a long weekend just the two of us."

"I'd love that."

"Why don't we go take a shower and get ready so we're not late?" I stood, and he locked his legs around my waist as I made my way upstairs to the master bathroom. I started the water and made sure it was the temperature he preferred then he dropped his legs, and I placed him under the spray.

I stepped back, and I watched him as he turned to wet his hair. I took in the water that cascaded down his frame. I bent over to untie my work boots. When I straightened, I caught his gaze, and I slowly stripped, he bit his lip as he studied me.

"Daddy?" he called my name as he poured shampoo in his palm.

"Yes, boy?"

"If I had been single before you enlisted, would you have told me how you felt?"

I pushed my underwear and pants off as I thought about

his question, but the answer was simple. "Yes. If you'd been single when I turned eighteen, I would've done everything to make you mine." I entered the stall and took over lathering his hair, working my fingers through the strands, massaging his scalp. "You were and are everything to me, Devon. Whether I was just Bern or Daddy, I'd want to spend the rest of my life with you. I know you're not ready yet, but someday you will be. Until then, I'll be right here."

I tipped his head back to strip the lather from his hair, and I saw in his eyes how much he wanted to give in, but I wanted him ready. He had years of neglect and shame to work through, and I knew he trusted me, but he didn't trust himself yet. All I could do was continue as I started showing him that he was all I'd ever needed.

I tenderly washed every inch of him and then let him do the same for me. He didn't touch my cock—he never did without permission. I know our relationship seemed odd to the outside world. He needed my domination and my caring. He depended on me to ground him. It was a part of me I'd never understood until him. Daddy was only ever for him. My gift to him alone.

We stole kisses until we finished our shower. Because it was my pleasure, I dried him and dressed him. I put on the suit he bought me. He shyly smiled up at me as he expertly knotted my tie. Through it all I touched him; it was an addiction. The thought of being without him now that I'd finally claimed him terrified me. Yearning for something—someone—so long and trying to tell yourself it wasn't meant to be to finally attaining it was hard to accept. As if just one jostle and I'd awaken, it would still be the secret dreams and fantasies I had of a life with him.

I wanted to hold on tightly and make demands, but I could only continue as I am.

"Ready?" I asked.

"Yes, I can't wait to introduce you to everyone. They've all mentioned how happy I've been the last few months."

"I want you to be happy."

I gave him one last kiss, and we left the house. I'd prefer to stay home with him all night, but I couldn't lock him away because of my selfishness. Although I didn't care where we were, I loved being with him. This weekend it would just be us in a cabin with no distractions and nothing to do but love on my boy.

13

DEVON

The breeze off the lake was chilly, and I wrapped Daddy's sweater around me and sipped my hot tea as he cleaned the kitchen. He'd told me to relax. I still couldn't get over what he'd done. *The cabin*. He'd made me my favorite meal. It was perfect. It was getting easier to process that he was mine, but it still felt like a dream. My co-workers and boss had loved him when I took him to the work dinner. I'd stood nearby when a lady from another floor asked who he'd come with and the pride when he'd pointed me out shocked me.

It shouldn't have though. My life was far different—I was different. I no longer looked at myself in shame. I'd accepted the pieces of me I'd kept hidden for thirty years. I stumbled, but Bern was always there to catch me. Some days I waited for my caution to push him away. He didn't fail to assure me that he'd be with me through the good and bad.

Strong arms encircled me, and I didn't hesitate to rest my weight against him.

"It's getting cold, boy, come inside, I started a fire for you."

A shiver worked up my spine as he led me inside without

releasing me. He kicked the door closed behind us, and that's when I noticed he'd moved the coffee table. Blankets and pillows were piled in its place.

"What's this?"

He removed the mug from my hands and unwrapped me from his sweater.

"Lift your arms."

I complied, and he removed my t-shirt. I glanced over my shoulder to catch him staring at me. His gaze followed the path of his fingertips. Goosebumps popped up on my arms. His intensity astounded me. When we were alone, his focus completely narrowed down to me. As if the world didn't exist beyond being with me. He stepped around me and knelt at my feet. He untied and removed my sneakers. He slipped off my socks and teased my instep, causing my toes to curl.

"Do you know what I thought the first time I saw you at my Dad's?"

I steadied myself by placing my hands on his shoulders as he started to undo my jeans.

"No."

"I had to ask myself how I could've stayed away from you for so long. That first hug was like coming home."

If I was supposed to speak, I couldn't have done so if my life depended on it. The truth of it was right there in his eyes as he looked up at me. All I could do was stand there as he stripped me bare physically and emotionally.

"You were as beautiful as the first time I realized I wanted you. I haven't been happy in the time I was away. I didn't understand that until I saw you waiting for me.

"Now, I want to ask you something."

I held my breath as he pulled something from his pocket. A small black bag sat in the palm of his hand.

"Take it."

My hands were shaking so badly that it took two tries to

pick up the bag. I worked the tiny drawstring loose. I hooked two rings with my finger and pulled them out. I studied them in silence. One had *Claimed* etched into the black surface of the thinner ring. I turned them to the light to find *Daddy* inside the band of one and *boy* in the other.

"You're not ready to marry me, and maybe we never will be, but that doesn't change the fact I want everyone to know you're mine and I'm yours. You were always meant to be my boy."

"Daddy..." My voice broke as he took the smaller ring and slowly slid it up the ring finger on my left hand. When he held up his hand for me, I felt the tears slipping faster down my cheeks.

"And if one day you don't want me to be Daddy and just plain old Bern, my feelings won't change. I loved you before I knew you needed a Daddy."

He straightened, and I didn't take my gaze off his as he swung me into his arms. His lips were firm and commanding, yet softened when he kissed away the tears from my cheeks. I held on tight as he lowered me to the makeshift bed in front of the fireplace.

"I'll always need a Daddy. I didn't understand what it was thirty years ago. But as I got older and realized, I felt embarrassed by it."

"And I told you there is no shame in what we want...what we do in our bed. Our needs are perfect for each other."

He stood and started removing his t-shirt, exposing his bulky muscles and hairy skin. I faintly noticed him toeing off his boots, but I was too distracted by him popping the button on his jeans. I rolled to my knees and sat back on my heels. When he pushed his pants down, I buried my face in his thick bush. Male musk and hints of soap. His hard cock nudged my chin, and the wet tip rubbed along the front of my neck. I whimpered, overwhelmed with need.

"My beautiful boy," he whispered, as he sweetly combed his fingers through my hair. Then I gasped as he fisted his hand in my hair and jerked me back. His free hand circled the base of his cock as he painted my lips with pre-cum. "Daddy aches so bad. You want to make him feel better, don't you?"

"Yes, Daddy." The minute he nudged my lips, I opened and tongued his loose foreskin, sucked it over the smooth head. He liked when I played with it, nibbled and sucked.

"Fuck, boy, you know how Daddy likes it. Do you play with yourself while you have dirty thoughts about your Daddy?"

I hummed as I eased my tongue beneath the skin and was rewarded with the taste of him. The skin teased my lips right before it receded as he stroked himself to pull the foreskin back. I didn't have time to prepare before he forced me to take every inch. My jaw ached as I tried to relax. He used my mouth as he saw fit. He showed no mercy. My cock painfully hardened as he choked me repeatedly, and then I was clawing at his hairy thighs as he tore himself away.

"Daddy, your boy needs it," I whined as I fought against his brutal grip.

"Daddy tells you what you need, boy." His features hardened as he chastised me and released my hair.

I stretched out on the blankets with my legs parted as I started to stroke my cock.

"Did you ask permission?"

I ignored his question as I stroked faster, panting as I kept my gaze on his cock. It seemed to jump each time I jacked my dick. His movements were angry as he finished removing his clothes, and he was suddenly kneeling beside me. I felt my head spin as I was turned over, forced to my knees, and the first strike took me by surprise.

"Boy, you do as your Daddy tells you." He had me recite the list of rules I'd memorized and the ones he'd added.

Tears flowed where my face was buried in my folded arms. Even in punishment, I felt loved, and a sense of peace came over me. As I recited the last rule, my muffled scream filled the room, as my lubed plug was slammed inside with no prep.

It was as if something shattered, and I was outside myself. I faintly realized he was turning me to my back. I was in a daze as he placed himself between my thighs and draped them to lie over his.

"Daddy only does what's best for you. I don't like punishing you. It hurts me more than you know."

His voice was soft, and then he was caressing me from thighs to chest. With each downward motion, he drew closer but never touched me where I needed him to. My hips arched as fingers just skirted my groin and he slowly massaged me, easing me down and I wrapped my hands around his wrists as he tweaked my trimmed pubes.

I begged and screamed as he loved on me by firelight. He sucked up marks to claim his ownership from my collarbones to my pelvis. I contracted around the plug that was nowhere near big enough to satisfy me. The sting of his love bites only teasing the pain I required.

"Daddy would leave you naked all the time. Are you ready to make Daddy feel good?"

"Please."

I was eased back to my knees and pulled back to straddle his thick thighs. He teasingly removed the plug and set it aside. I heard the snick of the lube cap, and then Daddy was right where I needed him. He curved his hands around my hips and urged me to take him.

"Show Daddy how you want me to fuck you."

I didn't need to be told twice. I worked on and off his dick in a frenzied pace. My cock slapped against my belly, and when my abused ass cheeks met his pelvis, pain exploded. And I almost came from it.

"Tell Daddy you want to be a good little boy."

"I'm a good boy, Daddy. You love fucking me?" I screamed as his hand landed on one cheek then the other.

"Always dreamed of fucking my boy's tight ass."

I barely noticed him shift and then he was over me, his mouth pressed to my ear and his left arm a steel band across my belly. I widened my stance and tipped my hips, and then we came together, we moved in perfect harmony.

"Daddy loves his boy taking his cock, dirty and unashamed."

I parted my lips, and he fucked needy sounds from me—my body wasn't mine. It had always belonged to him. He fucked me until my back arched upward under the assault of his hips. Burning pressure and just the right hint of pain, and I lowered myself until I stretched to grab a pillow and hug it against me. Burying my face in it. He placed his hand on the back of my head and pushed me deeper into it, each breath harder to draw in. I didn't panic or complain, I just let him deep stroke my ass in a savage pace as he jacked my cock.

"Take it, boy, I own you."

I threw my head back as I came so hard my head swam and screamed as I felt him filling me with his release. Grinding against me until I took it all. Sweat made my skin slick, and my heart was beating a frantic pace. I collapsed as I took his full weight, and he kept moving his hips.

"Daddy loves you, boy."

"I love you, too."

His hand in my hair turned my head until his lips could touch mine. "Say it again, Devon."

"I love you, Bern."

He hugged me tight, and I could feel his big smile against

my mouth. I whimpered as he slipped from me and turned us to our sides, and I completely relaxed against him.

"I will make sure you never regret trusting me with your heart."

"I know." And those two words came so easily, I trusted him without question. He would always keep every promise he'd make to me. He'd love me from now until our days together ended.

In the dancing shadows cast by the fire, I studied out joined hands. Our rings perfectly lined up and realized this was the one thing I'd always wanted, and it had been right there all along. I had no regrets or shame about who we were to each other. He'd be Daddy when I needed him, but also Bern. The sweet young man who'd taken care of me from afar until he knew I was free and the man who came home to claim me. And he didn't disrespect me or my need for that loving and controlling Daddy I'd secretly dreamed about but was so afraid to voice.

14

BERN

I was seated on the couch reading my paper one-handed while my boy curled against my side under my arm as he was on his e-reader. Occasionally I'd place a kiss on the crown of his head, and he'd nuzzle my bicep with his cheek. Each day, week, and month that passed only got better. Yes, we stumbled, couples fight. But I liked those too. Only because I knew he felt safe in voicing his opinion whether I agreed or not. He didn't back down, and he stood his ground, but deferred to me when it was something me as his Daddy thought was best.

"You two are joined at the hip every time I see y'all."

I laughed as I tipped my head back to see my dad entering the living room.

"Making up for lost time. What are you doing here? I thought you were going golfing or something with your old work buddies."

"Well..." He took a seat, and I knew he had something on his mind from the look in his eyes. "I was thinking about selling the house, moving someplace smaller and I wondered if you two would want it. It was the first purchase that your mom and I made together. It's paid off, and it was decided that when you got older and wanted your own home, it would go to you."

"We can buy it, Dad."

"No, it's your home. I didn't spend enough years with your mother in that house, but it's a home we built with love. You can consider it a claiming present or a wedding present whenever you two get around to it."

Dad wasn't subtle. He'd gotten excited when we'd returned from our cabin getaway with rings. I'd seen his disappointment when he found out we didn't elope. We'd explained that we didn't need some piece of paper to tell us we were married. We'd written wills and had power of attorney papers drawn up, we were all set, and neither of us felt the need to be parents. Dad had always known that I didn't want kids no matter the gender of the person I ended up with.

"But you love that house, Murray."

"I know, Devon, I do, and that's why I want you and Bern to have it. It's just me now, and I'd only held onto it to be closer to you and when my son came home. Now, it's just a place. Most of the memories I have there are amazing, but I really think it's time to move on. I've been looking at apartments, and my company asked if I would come back part-time to set up a new business here."

Dad had worked as a transition specialist for companies that were bought and resold. He helped the new offices with hiring and training. He'd traveled a lot with the job, and I remember he enjoyed the moving around.

"That will be great for you."

"Then you'll take it. As soon as I find an apartment, we can have the papers drawn up."

I sensed this was something he needed to do, and I respected his wishes. In his mid-fifties, he had time to start his life again and maybe moving away for a fresh start would be good for him. His loneliness was apparent, and when they'd offered him early retirement, he'd taken it because the money was too good. He felt more himself when he worked.

I released Devon as he got off the couch, and when he reached my dad, he gave him a hug. "We'd love to live in your house. There was always love there."

"It was, and I'll miss it, but Bern claimed you and found his happy. It's time for me to see about starting over. I don't see another love in my future, but work and friends, I miss all that."

"Mom would be proud."

"She would, and I miss her and will for the rest of my life, but she's been telling me for years in her videos to move on. Find happiness."

"Would you like to stay for dinner?" Devon asked as he returned to the spot beside me.

"No, I have to go and drag some clothes out that are appropriate for work. They want me to come in tomorrow to start planning the transition."

"Enjoy your first day at work and make sure you take lunch."

As I spoke, I saw the calm come over my dad. I knew I reminded him of Mom. He'd told me enough that I was all her best parts—the ones he'd loved the most. I was his reminder of her gift to him. I was the trigger for his greatest memories. He glanced at the mantle, and I followed it to the picture that had a place of honor beside mine and Devon's first picture.

Dad was seated on the floor, his head on my mother's thigh while she was pregnant with me, and she was stroking his hair just like I did for Devon. My dad's expression was one of peace and love, as if all was right with his world. His happiness was complete in that moment, and I wanted that for him again. Yet, I knew Dad would die still loving the odd woman who came up to him in a pub and told him he was hers.

I wanted my boy to view me like that. To think back in twenty or fifty years and want for nothing because the love we shared was complete.

Dad kissed us both on the forehead and then headed home. We stayed in silence for a few minutes as we were lost in our thoughts.

"We have a house, are you okay with that? I know we were looking for a place. If you'd rather have some place else, all you have to do is tell me," I offered.

"No, it's perfect. No house could come with more memories and love than that one. I know we briefly talked about redoing this one and staying. It wouldn't feel right. Like Murray, I want to start my life over, and there's no place more perfect."

"Your happiness means everything to me, boy."

"I know, Daddy, and this would mean the world to me."

"Then, it's a deal."

We sat on the couch late into the evening planning what to do with the things in his house and what we'd need for our new one. We worked out the details of the rest of our lives together. Dad losing Mom had taught me that we couldn't wait for tomorrow to come. I'd waited so long to make him mine. It hadn't set right with me, but I couldn't disrespect him by leading him in a direction that would've damaged our views of ourselves.

I no longer had to worry about that. We were free to live in the moment. We shared a light, late dinner, and then I carried him to bed. Tonight wasn't about sex, and I just held him, both of us were quiet as we savored our shared warmth.

"I love you, Devon."

"I love you too, Bern."

I turned him gently until he faced me. I drew his leg across my thigh as I closed the distance between our mouths. I kissed him as if I wouldn't awake in the morning. Told him I cared about him. I made sure he knew that I would be there when he stumbled or thought he wasn't good enough. Being his man—his Daddy—was what I was born to be. I'd always stand beside him and proudly show anyone who doubted us that their opinions didn't matter. I tucked his head under my chin as I tousled his hair the way he liked when I put him to sleep.

Calm came over me as his breaths evened out and he gave me his weight. His smooth skin flush to my hairier body. Two perfect halves and I could admit that if this hadn't of happened, I would have gone to my deathbed with the what-ifs of loving him.

But I wouldn't look back. All we could do was move forward, and we were whole because we were together. Devon and Bern. Daddy and Boy. Maybe one day husbands, but for now, what we had was perfect because it was completely us. I'd make sure that his love and trust were the greatest gifts I'd ever received.

EPILOGUE

DEVON

One Year Later

"Fuck boy," he growled behind me as he ruthlessly pounded my ass where I was leaned over the footboard of his childhood bed. His hand was over my mouth, and his lips met my ear. "Shhh, you want to get us caught? You don't want them to see your Daddy tearing your tight ass up. They wouldn't understand."

His words were low and dangerous. He'd denied my release over and over until the sway of my cock beneath me was enough to get me off.

"They wouldn't know you begged for Daddy's cock." He bit my shoulder. "Teased me into it." I whimpered at the hard smack of his hand on my hip. "My boy was naughty and needed to learn what he gets when he makes Daddy hard."

A full body shiver tightened all my muscles and my ass merciless squeezed my Daddy's cock. I didn't experience shame. This was us, what we craved; what I needed in order to be whole.

"Do you know how many times your Daddy fucked you in this bed?"

A horrifying muffled squeak caused my already burning cheeks to heat further. The headboard banged against the wall. It was loud in the whispered silence as we pretended we didn't want to get caught. This was the bed he'd jacked off to me and where he'd dreamed of owning me. His hands were rougher after months of working construction, so they almost abraded my skin. His heavy balls banged against mine as he measured himself in my tight hole.

"I came inside you a thousand times before I had the heaven of the real thing."

I protested as he jerked from me, spinning me so quickly my head spun and then I was back on his cock, slammed against his poster-covered wall beside the bed. Pictures rattled, and he used me, changed angles just enough to have me coming all over our bellies and then the real fucking began as he knew I'd come, it was his turn. He pinned my head against the wall with a hand around my throat, his face close enough for our breaths to mingle.

"You're gonna feel me until tomorrow."

The power of his thrusts forced me upward only to have me slam back down. I clawed at his arms and chest. His face was flushed and harsh as he fucked his boy as he dreamed of for all those years. His hips stuttered as he squeezed my throat tighter, and I felt it as he emptied himself into my hole.

Brutal to gentle in seconds as he eased me down with tender kisses and tear-inducing love words. I caught my breath when he stretched us out on his narrow bed. I used his chest for a pillow, and I pouted silently as he slipped free. His seed trickled down my taint and sac.

"I think we're going to keep this room as is, so I can show you all the ways I dreamed of you back then."

I giggled as he caressed my sides with the backs of his fingers. The aftermath with him was never rushed. It was soft words and tender touches, stolen kisses. Today was our one-year anniversary, and we'd finally moved into the house. Not a room was furnished, boxes were everywhere, but this room had been left just as he had the day he'd left for college.

I lifted my head and rested my chin on my crossed arms as I stared into his eyes. "Are you still happy with me?"

"More than when I came home and claimed you. Between us, in our bed and home, there's no shame. Your needs are my needs." He stroked my sweaty hair and lifted his head to give me a quick kiss.

"Did you know that I created this Daddy in my head for my fantasies? And everything about him was you. This man right here was the man I dreamed would take me in hand."

"Then, it was meant to be." He rimmed my stretched, cum-covered hole with his fingertips, and I lifted to take two thick digits.

"My slutty little boy doesn't care how Daddy fills him."

"As long as it's you."

"Until now and we draw our final breaths. I'm yours."

We understood that life could go pear-shaped at any time. We'd agreed to never take each other for granted. To never put off anything that needed to be said today. We whispered we loved each other at random times throughout the day. Kissed like it would be our last. Loved like we'd never be connected again. We loved without shame or the world's expectations.

He instructed me when needed. I'd lost count of the times I was ordered over his lap, but I also couldn't keep track of every touch he gave me simply because I was close enough to assure him that I was still there. I did the same for him.

"Daddy?" There was something I always wanted, and I

needed to ask Daddy first. "I wanted to ask you something important."

"Yes, boy." He gifted me with an adoring gaze.

"I want a puppy."

"What my boy wants, my boy gets." He just smiled and cuddled me closer.

I spun my ring with my thumb. It was my reminder when I was away from him that I was claimed. I belonged. I didn't have to be anything but me and his boy. My imperfect, middle-aged body was sexy because it was his. My anxiety and insecurities weren't wrong because they were a part of me. He loved every part, even the ones that weren't ideal. His love was never less than a hundred percent.

THE END

ABOUT THE AUTHOR

J.M. Dabney is a multi-genre author who writes mainly LGBT romance and fiction. They live with a constant diverse cast of characters in their head. No matter their size, shape, race, etc. J.M. lives for one purpose alone, and that's to make sure they do them justice and give them the happily ever after they deserve. J.M. is dysfunction at its finest and they makes sure their characters are a beautiful kaleidoscope of crazy. There is nothing more they want from telling their stories than to show that no matter the package the characters come in or the damage their pasts have done, that love is love. That normal is never normal and sometimes the so-called broken can still be amazing.

ALSO BY J.M. DABNEY

Sappho's Kiss Series

When All Else Fails

More Than What They See

Dysfunction it its Finest Series

Club Revenge

Soul Collector Prophecy

Twirled World Ink Series

Berzerker

Trouble

Scary

Lucky

Brawlers Series

Crave

Psycho

Bull

Hunter

Executioners Series

Ghost

Joker

King

Sin & Saint

Trenton Security

Livingston

Little

Gage

Pure (Coming Summer 2019)

Masiello Brothers

The Taming of Violet

3 Moments Trilogy

A Matter of Time

The Men of Canter Handyman

Black Leather & Knuckle Tattoos

Chance at the Impossible

Bloody Knuckles Bar & Grill

Clipping the Gargoyle's Wings

New West City Universe

Co-written with Davidson King

The Hunt

Standalone

By Way of Pain (Criminal Delights - Assassins)

Printed in Great Britain
by Amazon

87045359R00073